The Villagers

The Villagers

A.J. Griffiths - Jones

Published 2016 by Creativia
Paperback design by Creativia (www.creativia.org)
ISBN: 978-1530037070
Cover art base image by Sylvia Caswell
Cover design by http://www.thecovercollection.com/
This book is a work of fiction. Names, characters, places, and incidents are the product of the author's imagination or are used fictitiously. Any resemblance to actual events, locales, or persons, living or dead, is purely coincidental.

For Olive

Author's Note

The events, characters and places portrayed in this novel are loosely based upon the real lives of people who resided in and around a small village in England in the 1950's. However, I have used some imagination in recreating the series of events and have changed the names of those involved.

The main character is my beloved grandmother who, at ninety-six years old, has spent many an afternoon retelling to me the story of her time in an idyllic cottage in that hamlet. We have laughed until we cried and when the time came for me to put pen to paper to create this piece of fiction, many memories, both good and bad, were stirred up in the process. Unfortunately, my grandfather Geoff is no longer with us but I'm sure that he is looking down now and having a good old chuckle about the place that he used to call home.

As you follow 'The Villagers' through their individual journeys, remember that truth is very often stranger than fiction and, although this is a novel and the story created for your entertainment, there is an element of truth in each of these lives. Olive herself would tell you that.

In creating this book, I owe thanks to several people without whom I would have struggled to accurately portray the story that will gradually unfold before you. Firstly, I send my love to my grandmother, and hope that she will have as much pleasure reading this story as we did creating it, she is truly wonderful and I hope that when I'm old and grey I will be just as enthusiastic about life as she has always been.

For the second time in my writing career, I am indebted to Sylvia and Antony Caswell. Sylvia spent many hours creating a superb oil painting from which Antony has been able to create the cover of 'The Villagers', from very little more than an inspired idea. You are both so immensely talented.

To Lesley Mitchell and Ashley Scott, without the two of you Chapter Seven wouldn't exist.

Recognition to Phil Carter in Norway for his constructive criticism, honest review & ongoing support.

I would also like to thank my dear friend Sarah Locker, who not only read the whole manuscript and provided much needed feedback, but also endured me reading out passages to her while we lounged on sunbeds in Turkey, just so that I could gage her reaction. Your support is much appreciated.

Finally, to my husband Dave, who is always there to provide both physical and emotional support, says nothing when I get up in the middle of the night to scribble down ideas and every now and again comes up with a genius idea, words will never be enough to tell you how very much you mean to me.

Contents

Prologue

With every cherished memory, there is a beautiful, tranquil, idealistic place that, when recalled to mind, can transport you back to the innocence of your childhood. These were the towns and hamlets where dreams were made, friendships moulded, hearts broken and personalities forged.

Everyone has one of these places, no matter how long ago or how short the stay, a place that makes them warm inside and brings a momentary tug at their heartstrings. Somewhere safe that creates a sensual feeling and brings tears to our eyes when those long forgotten heroes are once again replayed in our fading recollections.

The characters we met, some long gone to their graves, many of them old and grey, and some who simply disappeared without a trace, these are the people that made growing up such fun. There are always the amusing ones whose names we can never recall and the grumpy ones whose names trip off our tongues so easily, right up until our senior years. Take a moment to reflect upon these people. The kind but strict schoolmaster urging you to always do better, the crazed old lady who would wave a stick from inside her cat-ridden house when she caught you trying to scrump apples from her orchard, the cheerful postman who would willingly battle hail and snow to bring letters and cards from loved ones overseas and the portly shopkeeper who would always sneak a few extra toffees into the bag when you laid your last pennies on his counter.

In these wonderful places, it wasn't about the buildings. Concrete and stone had no part in making us the individuals that we would become. No, it was the flesh and blood, the friends, neighbours and casual passers-by with whom we would build forever friendships, acquaintances and fond, fond memories. In our childhood homes we were safe, protected and above all happy. We were cocooned from the outside world by a tight network of people, who seemed to want no more than to nurture our souls.

Places like these filled every corner of post-war Britain, beautiful communities with chocolate-box cottages and smiling children everywhere, a safe haven where doors were left unlocked and children rode their bicycles for miles without a care. Clusters of houses where people shared their troubles and rallied around to help a neighbour in need, baking pies for the elderly, concocting home remedies for the sick and pulling together to make the community function as a whole, wanting nothing in return.

And then there was 'The Village'.

Chapter One
Olive and Geoff

It was the summer of 1950 when Olive and Geoff moved to the village.

Neither of them could imagine a more picturesque and peaceful location in which to bring up their three young children, a haven of tranquility and calm, a place in which to nurture their family and grow old gracefully together. Surrounded by beautiful Shropshire country-side, with rolling hills on all directions, a better location would have been impossible to find. Parents had few worries about passing traffic in those quiet lanes and allowed their off-spring to play freely on the footpaths and fields nearby. The few vehicles that did pass through the village did so slowly and cautiously, their drivers as much on the lookout for roaming foxes crossing their pathways as children picking berries in the hedgerows. The houses were solid and well-made, the gardens obviously tended with loving care. Each frontage had a little latched gate and each doorway was surrounded by a cascade of fragrant roses. Retired folk sat chatting on the benches of the village green, tractors hummed busily in the surrounding fields and sparkling white linens blew merrily in the wind on the washing-lines of every household.

The other people in the village seemed to be decent, friendly and respectable. Every Sunday as the church bell tolled, a steady stream of parishioners made their way up the long and winding pathway that led to the grand Norman church at the end of the thoroughfare. Ancient tombstones lined the grass verges on all sides, some erect as steel, some tipping sideways with age and decay. These were the markers of many generations of villagers, some of them spanning half a millennium. To one side there stood a few grand tombs, obviously the final resting places of the more wealthy villagers from days gone by, but most of the markers were simple burial places inscribed with little more than names and dates. Despite the lapse of time, each and every one of them bore a small posy of flowers at its base, signifying that the long dead resident was very much alive in the heart of his or her descendants. This was a place where few people left and new residents only came after childless generations had passed away, leaving empty properties to be sold by the state. Olive knew that her friends would do anything to move to this village, but fate had smiled down on her, and her only. This was a golden opportunity.

Day to day life was comparable to that of any small community. The men of the village went off to work every morning, by bicycle, motorbike, bus and car, returning at dusk to a smiling wife and happy children. Their cottages were filled with the smells of freshly baked pies and homemade bread, with beautiful wild flowers adorning scrubbed kitchen tables and welcoming fires in the grates. To any onlooker passing through, the village was a hub of contentment and serenity, a place that city-dwellers could only dream of and a constant attraction for families seeking a place in which to enjoy a picnic in peaceful solitude.

Olive and Geoff's cottage was perfect. It looked out on to the rest of the properties from a prime location at the end of a quiet cul-de-sac and needed very little to be done before the family could move in their possessions. There were two good-sized bedrooms and a little box-room which would be ideal for baby Godfrey. The two girls would share and Geoff had spent the whole weekend, before the move, painting the walls an inviting shade of sunshine yellow to make it look bright and airy. The large sitting room had an open fireplace and plush sage green carpet, whilst the kitchen-diner was large enough for the family to sit comfortably over their evening meals. Geoff had already started planning all the things he was going to make in his new garage, there was even room for a wood-turning lathe which would be ideal for making some unique toys for the children. Olive had polished, scrubbed and buffed the cottage from top to bottom and, thanks to the generosity of her mother, brilliant white net curtains now hung from every window. She planned to grow herbs and a few vegetables in the rear garden, maybe even buy a few ducks or chickens, it just seemed the right thing to do in the countryside. Olive was more than content. This was going to be a wonderful place to live.

As Geoff brought in the last box of crockery from his little Austin car, Olive simultaneously busied herself with unpacking, making a pot of tea and rocking the baby in his pram. Today was the beginning of a long and happy life in the country, she could feel it in her bones. The two girls, Eileen and Barbara were already out exploring the village on their bicycles and at the ages of ten and eight respectively they were just as excited as their parents at the prospect of making new friends and putting down firm roots. Baby Godfrey was only a few months old but gurgled happily as Olive pushed him outside into the bright sunlight. Even he seemed delighted to be in the village,

That evening, as they sat down to tea, the little family raised their teacups in celebration of their new home. Olive and Geoff were quick to quiz their daughters on how they felt about the move, but any fears they might have had were ungrounded and both girls seemed to approve of their new home wholeheartedly. Apparently Eileen had already made a new friend and Barbara, a feisty bad-tempered child, had found an enemy in the delicate blonde girl two doors down. There would be plenty of scrapes and arguments with that one, mused Olive, Barbara really should have been born a boy. Eileen would cause little trouble, of that her mother had no doubt, but the other one would need watching like a hawk as mischief always followed her around like a hungry stray dog. Barbara had even argued with her elder sister over which bed she wanted to sleep in and had created such a fuss that eventually Geoff had rearranged the beds so that both of his daughters would be lying facing the window. Barbara was such a handful and her mother secretly longed for the summer holidays to end so that the teachers could take dual responsibility for disciplining her, but for now she would be allowed to run wild in the fields every day in the hope that by teatime her energy would be completely used up.

Later that night, as they lay in bed between fresh cotton sheets, Olive and Geoff reflected on the kindness of their neighbours. Throughout the day, a steady stream of faces had appeared at the kitchen window, all of them bearing gifts and none of them outstaying their welcome. There had been freshly baked bread from a rather red-faced lady in a flowered apron, a dozen fresh eggs from the young man next door, pots of jam and chutney from the vicar's wife and a large jug of warm milk, fresh from the cowshed, courtesy of the local farmer. Olive couldn't remember all of their names but vowed to get to know them and therefore become an integral part of village life.

The first few years of their married lives had been spent living in a rent-free two-bedroomed farm cottage owned by Geoff's parents, which had helped them to save enough money to put down the deposit on their own home, something for which the couple would be eternally grateful. Geoff had enjoyed being close to his family but as it became more and more apparent that he no longer wanted to follow in his father's footsteps and instead veered his mind towards the exciting world of invention and engineering, a break from the close-knit smallholding seemed inevitable.

"Who was the lady with the rosy cheeks and pink lipstick?" asked Geoff, turning to face Olive who was moisturising her face in the vanity mirror, "She makes a grand crusty loaf."

"I think she lives next door but one. She was very friendly", replied Olive, "Isn't it lovely when people rally round to make sure you've got something on the table for your first night's tea?"

"It certainly is, my dear."

"Geoff, are you happy we've moved?" Olive asked cautiously, glancing at her husband's reflection behind her, "I mean, away from your family?"

"Don't ask daft questions", tutted Geoff, "Now, get in to bed, and start dreaming about all those hours of gossiping and cups of tea you've got to get through as you come to know everyone."

Olive put down the pot of cream and sauntered over to her side of the bed. She climbed in and sighed.

Geoff was right, as usual, and within minutes the couple had drifted off to sleep.

There would be plenty of time for reflection on their move later.

There was a market town about five or six miles away from their new location and Olive had seen the ladies of the village boarding the local bus to take them shopping on Thursdays and Saturdays. That would be an ideal way of getting to know her fellow inhabitants and perhaps, after filling her basket with local produce, she could sit with them over a pot of tea before boarding the bus back home. Olive had it all planned out, and looked forward to the day when she would be familiar with the cheerful faces living around her. She daydreamed of village fetes, coffee mornings and flower-arranging at the local church. Some of the ladies in the village had already perked Olive's interest, and she was sure that friends would be made by the dozen.

Olive and Geoff's first few weeks in the village were taken up with emptying boxes, settling the two girls in to their new school and finding out all the necessary information required to live in the countryside, such as delivery days for the greengrocer and bread van, church service times and the schedule of the local bus services to town. Of course Geoff also had his job at the foundry, where he worked as a patternmaker, so Olive dashed here and there making their new home a place to relax in. Relatives had been to visit in abundance, everyone wanting to know how life was treating them in the village, and Olive's two brothers had stayed for a few days to help paint doors and put up shelves. During that time the little cottage had been full of laughter, singing and continued bustle as the two men busied themselves from morning till night. They would do anything for Olive, their most amenable sister, and both had a lot of time for their brother-in-law too. As far as they were concerned, a few days off work spent helping

Olive and Geoff to fix up their new home was well worth it just to see the smiles on their faces. Her three sisters had also paid a visit. Phoebe the eldest had been helpful and kind, bringing sweets for the children and taking care of baby Godfrey for a few hours so that Olive could continue to organise her new home. Next had come Dolly, the joker of the family, providing respite from her sister's busy day as she poured tea and told tales of the friends that Olive had left behind. The two sisters had laughed uncontrollably on many occasion and vowed to make sure that the distance in miles that now lay between them would do nothing to stop them from enjoying each other's company on a regular basis.

Lastly, Olive's youngest sister Minnie had alighted from the small green bus, resplendent in her new straw hat and impractical three inch heels. Olive laughed inwardly as Minnie manoeuvred her way along the dusty path, all the while trying desperately to look chic. Of all her sisters, Minnie was the most difficult to get along with and caused constant friction with her siblings, but even the three-hour long visit to her sister's new home, eyeing up every nook and looking for fault in every cranny, could do nothing to dampen Olive's high spirits. As she walked her sister to the bus-stop Olive took a deep breath and said thanks. Life in the village had calmed her beyond belief.

The hustle and bustle of settling in had left very little time to get acquainted with the neighbours but, slowly and surely, as the weeks passed, and as opportunity presented itself, Olive came to know the residents of the village.

Unfortunately she also found out their secrets.

Of course every family has secrets, but as the days, weeks and years passed by, Olive would gradually come to know every skeleton in every closet. Sometimes she dearly wished that things had remained hidden, that the occupants of the village had not openly revealed to her their sins and obsessions. Some things were best kept behind closed doors. It wasn't as if Olive actively sought to help or counsel the villagers around her, in fact she dearly wished that she could have continued her life of ignorance as far as their sordid conspiracies were concerned. It seemed that everyone knew and accepted the terrible deeds going on around them, a secret society where all were aware but nobody told. The village was shrouded in guilt, loathing and desire.

As any wife would do, as each secret revealed itself, Olive shared her newfound knowledge with her husband. Geoff merely laughed. Poor Olive must be bored out here in the country, he thought, too much fresh air is affecting her imagination. Of course when his dear wife started to lose sleep Geoff worried a little but put it down to the change in environment or the time of the month, sometimes he even blamed it on the full moon. Occasionally he would hear Olive put on her dressing-gown and creep downstairs to make a cup of tea, but Geoff had a hard day at work ahead and the temptation of a warm bed and soft pillow were enough to ease him back into slumber. At other times he would awake to hear his wife's shallow breathing and knew that she was laying still, eyes fixed on the ceiling, trying not to give any clues that she had been without sleep for hours. Naturally Geoff cared, but he knew full well how people's minds could play tricks on them. Geoff was certain that Olive would eventually settle down to her new life and stop fretting over the things she thought she'd witnessed. After all, he pondered, some of the things she had told him were almost impossible to believe, it was almost as if Olive were reliving some kind of nightmare from her childhood. It would pass, and soon she would come to her senses, he thought.

But there lay the problem. You see, the things that Olive saw and heard were all too real.

Chapter Two
Anna & Wolfgang Muller

Anna Muller was an elegant and bold woman, with strong equine features and an enviable wardrobe. She was proud of her Russian heritage but strove to improve her English in order to fit in with the little community in which she lived. It was important to Anna that the villagers accept her, especially as there had been a general distrust of all foreigners seeking refuge in England both during and after the war. Now in the third year of her residency in the village, Anna was still very much aware of the awe in which others looked at her every time she opened her mouth. But it wasn't just her strong St. Petersburg accent that drew their attention. If Anna had looked around her, she would have seen that it was her statuesque figure and sleek raven hair that caused people to stop and stare. The village women were envious of her high cheekbones and flawless complexion often stopping Anna, as she entered the village shop or made her way to church, for advice on everything from night creams to hair conditioners.

Her Polish husband was a much less memorable figure and rather reminded one of a shy dormouse just emerging from a long winter of hibernation. He wasn't a small man by any means but, being several inches shorter than his wife, Wolfgang Muller appeared to be of slight stature as he walked alongside the beautiful Anna. Nobody knew how long the Muller's had been married, but neighbours wondered if or when the couple would have children. Of course nobody ever asked, as the pair seemed to prefer to keep to themselves and besides, it wasn't the sort of question that you could ask in passing.

Despite their lack of day to day interaction with the other villagers, the Muller's were regular church-goers and never missed a Sunday service. They also attended the fund-raising activities in the local district, and could be relied upon to provide unwanted items for the 'White Elephant' stall at the fete or bottles of homemade wine to be sold for a good cause. Wolfgang Muller was becoming quite a well-known name when it came to festive tipples, with such creations as mulberry and cinnamon, elderflower and rosehip, and his most revered dandelion and juniper. The villagers always looked forward to purchasing his wonderful array of alcoholic beverages at Christmas, not in the least because Wolfgang offered a generous sample glass for every interested customer, which was always accompanied by one of his wife's exquisite ginger biscuits. Nobody seemed to mind that the couple had no interest in forging solid friendships, it was simply accepted that they both had a different social upbringing to the English folk around them and they were left to their own devices.

Of course, there were always the curious ones who would while away the hours in idle chatter, pondering how the meek little Polish man with his milk-bottle lenses had managed to snare the tall and refined Russian beauty, but nobody dared to pry. Besides, sometimes it was much more fun to let both the imagination and the gossip run wild. Nobody meant any harm, and the whole village was unanimous in their respect for the foreigners wanting to keep their married life private. It was with a mild curiosity that curtains twitched as Wolfgang Muller left his house at exactly the same hour every morning, come rain or shine. Nobody seemed to know his profession or why he was always seen wearing a pristine business suit, even at the weekends. He would trot down the path at a brisk pace with a brown paper bag containing his lunch gripped tightly in one hand and a long black gentleman's umbrella in the other. However, the villagers were even more interested in Anna Muller, who would appear an hour later, furtively glancing around her as she closed her front door, looking as beautiful and radiant as ever in her navy raincoat and red paisley silk headscarf. Monday to Friday, she would head off down the lane to the bus-stop and not return until an hour before her husband later in the day.

The Muller's front door was painted a deep shade of forest green, with the brass knocker and handles having been polished until you could quite clearly see your reflection in them. The front lawn was a decent but manageable size, with marigolds and dahlias planted neatly around the border, and a cascading rose bush taking pride of place in the very centre of the immaculately mown grass. Every window in the house was dressed in pure white plain net curtains, preventing passers-by from getting even the slightest glimpse inside, which only resulted in the people of the village becoming more inquisitive about their secretive neighbours. Even the postman had commented on the Muller's lack of letters from their relatives overseas, they were destined, so he thought, to be loners.

At the weekends, the Mullers conducted their household maintenance in much the same manner as every other couple in the village. Mr. Muller would pull his battered old manual lawnmower out of the shed and carefully stride up and down cutting the grass, after which he would tirelessly pull out any weeds which had found their way in to the borders and then take out a set of wooden ladders in order to give the front windows a good clean. Meanwhile, if you watched for long enough, slight glimpses of Anna could be seen hanging out washing, beating her intricately designed Persian rugs on the back doorstep and carefully setting out washed milk bottles ready for collection. However, unlike the carefree females who peered at her with intrigue from the confines of their own little cottages, not a hair could be found out of place on Anna's head, her white pinafore was crisp and starched and silk stockings adorned her slim, shapely legs as she worked. Many a conversation at the village shop had been centered upon the amount of time it must have taken the dignified Russian to get ready every morning, with figures ranging from two to six hours. The overall consensus was that such a well-manicured and groomed lady must either never sleep or she had a personal beautician on hand to preen her to perfection.

The Muller's neat little house was just two doors away from Olive and Geoff's and being in such close proximity, you would have expected the two couples to have become quite well acquainted but, as it was, a quick greeting at the gate and a wave from the garden were pretty much all that was exchanged. In such rural areas as the village it was common for people to borrow tools, exchange cake recipes and to offer their services to neighbours in need, but the Muller's kept their door closed, their garden gate shut and their personal business to themselves. All that the villagers had managed to glean from them in three years was Anna and Wolfgang's nationalities, despite their surname sounding very decidedly un-Polish, and the fact that they both enjoyed classical music. This was confirmed each and every Sunday afternoon, when the dulcet tones of Mozart and Beethoven could faintly be heard coming from the Muller's gramophone. It seemed that the couple were financially comfortable, but nobody had ever so much as peeked through their front door, so no-one actually knew in what style the Muller's lived. Olive thought it a pity that her closest neighbours weren't a little more sociable, especially as they were of a similar age to her and Geoff, but she was on friendly terms with plenty of others in the village and was happy to let it be.

However, all that changed one September when Olive's eldest daughter started senior school and needed to travel in to town on the local bus.

Eileen had always been a gifted child, therefore Olive and Geoff's decision to send her to an all-girls secondary school where she could focus on her studies without teenage boys to distract her was nothing of a surprise to their friends and family. They had high hopes for Eileen and wanted the very best education possible for her. A half hour journey each way on the local bus was a small sacrifice to make and, besides, Eileen was both sensible and mature enough to make the trip on her own. Also, the driver was a cheerful and conscientious local man and would ensure that Olive's daughter was safely delivered to her destination. Unfortunately the same could not be said of Barbara's academic status, and despite their other daughter still having two more years in junior school, it had already been decided that she would be enrolled in to the state comprehensive with the rest of the village children.

It was only after a couple of weeks of travelling back and forth to her new school that Eileen became aware of another regular passenger following the same route. Day after day, Anna Muller would be waiting at the bus-stop in her smart navy mackintosh and sensible shoes, clutching her handbag and a brown paper parcel. Every morning she would be looking eagerly up and down the lane, head held high and silk scarf tied neatly under her chin, awaiting transport to the market town. Eileen always politely said hello and Mrs. Muller always smiled back at her in response.

Eileen noticed that her neighbour alighted at the same stop every day, just on the outskirts of town near the park, and was waiting at that exact spot on the return journey after school. Eileen wasn't a mischievous girl and had no intention of letting her curiosity get the better of her, although she knew very well that her younger sister would have played detective and followed Mrs. Muller with the intent of discovering what pursuits filled her hours every day. As time passed, Eileen became preoccupied with her studies, making dozens of new friends and slowly coming to terms with the increasing amount of homework that she needed to complete each evening. Weeks turned in to months and the summer gave way to autumn winds and cold showers. Still Anna Muller made her journey in to town, the only change being the addition of a sweater under her coat and a pair of leather gloves covering her perfectly manicured hands.

Eventually Eileen could bear the suspense no longer and resolved to find out the reason for Mrs. Muller's continuous trips. For a young girl it was deeply puzzling. Should Anna Muller not be at home baking bread and doing laundry like mother? Did she have enough time to prepare an evening meal for her husband after being out all day long? Did Mrs. Muller have a sick relative for whom she needed to care every day? Or could it possibly be the unthinkable and she was having an affair? One morning Eileen had confided her suspicions in her best friend while they played hopscotch in the schoolyard, but unfortunately, Gloria had in turn become convinced that Anna Muller was a spy. It was quite common for women to pretend to be house-wives during the war, whilst secretly penetrating top government se-crets, Gloria had told her. Besides, she continued, from the description of Mrs. Muller it was highly unlikely that such a glamorous foreign woman would be innocently living in the English countryside. Eileen had no such thoughts and the two girls had quarreled continuously for the whole duration of their lunch break. It was the first time that Eileen had ever shouted at her friend, and she spent the rest of the week avoiding the subject of Anna Muller's origins, and concentrated her efforts instead on winning back her best friend. However, the ques-tion of the Russian's movements still bothered her, therefore the only way for Eileen to stop tormenting herself was to simply ask.

Raising the question itself was the hardest part but, one cold and windy day after a particularly difficult geography lesson, Eileen plucked up the courage to delve into the mystery. Therefore that mis-erable afternoon, as Anna Muller climbed on to the little green bus, Eileen edged forward from her place at the rear and slid onto the seat behind her neighbour. At first Eileen gave a short cough but it failed to create a response, so the young girl took the bold step of tapping Mrs. Muller gently on the shoulder.

Anna Muller turned around slowly, her shining dark eyes taking in the pretty blonde girl behind her like a crow surveying its prey. But instead of asking what it was that Eileen wanted, the genteel Russian merely tapped the leather seat beside her and slid towards the window, gesturing with a slight incline of the head for Eileen to join her. Anna was curious, this pretty child from the village was courteous and meek.

At first the two sat in companionable silence, neither looking at the other but both feeling inquisitive and shy. The town gave way to countryside and the bus made several stops to allow passengers to either jump on or depart. It was the older woman who finally broke the silence.

'Did you have a good day at school?' she asked, the words tripping faultlessly off her tongue.

'Yes, thank you, well apart from having to learn the name of every ocean and sea from here to China, which I really don't see the point of', replied Eileen, immediately feeling slightly embarrassed that she had shared such a trivial bugbear. She stared down at her hands, wondering if the lady at her side thought her a fool.

'Oh, but it's very important to know where the waters lead to', came the response, 'One day you may feel the wish to travel and see the world, then you will definitely need to know where the oceans go'.

Eileen thought for a moment. It seemed that not only was Mrs. Muller attractive but she was wise too.

"Have you travelled a lot, Mrs. Muller?"

"Not too much", said Anna, dismissing the question with a wave of the hand, "But you are still very young and have your whole life ahead of you. The world is your oyster."

'I suppose you're right', replied the schoolgirl, 'Did you have a good day?'

Eileen wasn't sure but she thought that she felt her new friend stiffen at the question, nothing too drastic but just a momentary arch of her shoulders. Whatever the emotion behind the sudden twinge, it was gone within seconds and a smile slowly spread across the Eastern European's bow-shaped lips.

'Yes, thank you', nodded Anna, 'I suppose I did have a good day today'.

With a short nod of the head, Mrs. Muller then turned to look out of the window, lost in her thoughts and now oblivious to the child at her side. The conversation was over.

That evening Eileen lay in front of the roaring fire, her homework books lying redundant on the rug in front of her, thoughts a million miles away. What a stylish and chic lady Mrs. Muller is, she mused, and she has such good English for a foreigner, although Eileen had never actually met a non-English person before and had nobody else to compare the elegant Russian's language skills with. She reached forward and drew the hard-backed atlas towards her. Now how many seas would you cross to get to Russia? she pondered.

"What's that you've got there then?"

Eileen looked up to see her father stooping down to look at the map. She explained her conversation with Anna Muller earlier that day and how she was now counting the different seas between their own little island and the vast country from which the lady next door but one hailed.

Geoffrey nodded wisely and settled back on the sofa.

"Russia played a big part in the war", he explained, "Sit up here and I'll tell you all about it."

Eileen listened eagerly as her father recounted tales of Hitler, outlined with his finger the countries whose men had fought alongside their British allies and the harsh conditions endured by the Russian soldiers as they had marched towards the battlefront. As a pattern-maker for Rolls Royce aircraft engines, Geoff's job had been deemed important to the war effort and he had been excluded from enlistment, much to Olive's relief, but Eileen could see that he was just as patriotic and informed about it as those who had fought under Winston Churchill's orders. Her father had a gift for making stories come to life and that night a spark was lit in the young girl's mind, prompting her to borrow cultural books from the library and to raise her hand persistently in geography class at school. Russia seemed so very far away to a young girl who's most adventurous trip had been a family outing to the coast in North Wales. Never before had Eileen encountered such enchanting buildings as the cathedrals and palaces that graced the picture books on Eastern Europe. It was another world, one where princesses and tsarinas danced in gilded ballrooms and drank tea from golden samovars. One day, when she was grown up, Eileen would go there to see for herself she decided. For now, she would have to be content with flicking through the pages of her battered atlas and making regular trips to the library in town to satisfy her curiosity. Of course it would have been much easier to ask Anna Muller to tell her all about Russia, but Eileen was unsure whether the woman's home country would hold fond memories for her or not. After all, if she had been happy there, why come to live in England?

As October winds turned to November rain, Eileen's daily journeys became filled with intrigue. It became a regular habit for her to sit closer to the front of the bus, and every day her neighbour would gesture for the child to board the vehicle ahead of her and, without hesitation, Mrs. Muller took the seat next to Eileen. Usually no more than a few words were exchanged between the young girl and the beautiful Russian but slowly and surely an invisible trust was forged between the two and Eileen shared her frustrations and dreams. In turn the mystery of Mrs. Muller's regular trips to town gradually began to unravel.

At first, when Eileen learned the true reason behind Anna Muller's daily routine, she was both disappointed and confused. It seemed that her elegant friend did little more than sit in the park, feeding the ducks and pigeons with bread from her small brown package. Apparently Mrs. Muller hated confined spaces and rather than spend her days cooped up at home, preferred to sit on a bench with only fresh air and feathered friends to disturb her thoughts. Eileen couldn't understand the appeal. Some days were so damp and miserable that even the heated classroom barely warmed her through. Still, each to their own devices, she thought, hoping that her new friend wouldn't catch a chill sitting in the open air all day. What a strange way to spend your day, the youngster mused, she must be there for over six hours, with nobody to talk to, nothing to read and the chance of rain looming all the time. Eileen wondered if Mrs. Muller had told her the truth. What if Gloria had been right all along and her foreign friend was up to something? The county's council offices were located overlooking the park, perhaps Anna waited in the park for one of its officers to furtively pass her some secret information? But then again, surely a bigger borough or even a city would have far more classified files than this little market town. Eileen could quite clearly imagine the scenario taking place, with the elegant Russian sitting waiting on a park bench, a tall handsome gent in a light coloured trench coat casually walking past, and then stooping down to tie his shoelace as he approached the bench. As he bent over, the man would deftly drop a slip of paper next to the woman's foot, where she would quickly cover it with her shoe, waiting to retrieve it when the man had completely disappeared from view. Or wait, was that the scene of a Hollywood movie that she had seen at the cinema with her Aunt Dolly? Whatever the case, thought Eileen, feeding birds in the park every day certainly wasn't fun so there must be more to it than Anna Muller had revealed.

And then, one afternoon, everything changed.

Eileen had been ill at home for a week, nothing serious, just a stomach bug, but it was enough for her mother to insist on full bed rest and regular doses of hasty pudding, a sugary and milky concoction that Olive believed was the answer to all ailments. Poor Eileen was bored being stuck in the house and missed her school friends desperately. She also missed her regular chats with Anna Muller. Every morning, as the youngster sat at the kitchen table eating her toast and jam, she had craned her neck to watch the tall, mysterious foreigner hurry down the lane to catch the bus. Olive had laughed at her daughter on a few occasions, and took her interest in Mrs. Muller to be no more than that of a child taking her first steps towards a love of fashion. After all, the immaculate Anna Muller was extremely well turned-out, with never a loose button or fraying cuff to mar her trim and stylish outfits. At the few events in the village that Olive had seen her neighbours dress up in their best frocks, the tall Russian had always out-shone them all. In a very humble but effective manner, Mrs. Muller had arrived sporting a simple but classic dress, with perfectly coifed hair, and just the right amount of lipstick and rouge. It was with great amusement that Olive had witnessed other ladies in the vicinity trying to emulate Anna's impeccable style, but with a far lesser degree of success. Either they lacked the Russian woman's curvaceous bone structure, failed to control their hair with grips or quite simply smeared on the blusher as though using a trowel.

On the day that Eileen returned to school, she earnestly looked forward to seeing her neighbour and was delighted to see the tall, handsome woman waiting at the bus-stop as usual. A smile played on the Russian's lips, as though she too had been looking forward to this meeting.

'Are you feeling better?' asked Mrs. Muller.

'Yes, much', replied Eileen 'But how did you know I was ill?'.

'Oh, it's not very hard to work out', replied the older woman 'If a schoolgirl misses her lessons for a week during term time, there is usually only one reason behind it'.

Eileen nodded, it didn't take a genius to work that out, but that was also exactly the type of reasoning that a spy would use when trying to work out something about their enemy. She looked up at the woman by her side to see if she could detect anything more going on behind her dark eyes and rigid features but saw nothing more than someone genuinely showing concern.

"I'm looking forward to going back to school", she said, "I've missed a lot of lessons."

"You'll catch up in no time", Mrs. Muller replied, "Of that, I have no doubt at all."

Eileen blushed. She felt that the compliment had been heartfelt and genuine.

A few minutes later the little green bus arrived, whisking its passengers along the winding lanes and creating a loud hum over which Eileen and her friend exchanged pleasantries. Anna Muller commented on the weather and how the evenings were becoming darker much earlier week by week, while Eileen shared the names of books that she had read while at home recovering from her illness. For the young girl, this was the first time that she had encountered an adult who had never read the Bronte sisters novels or entered the glorious world of Dicken's characters and she enjoyed outlining the stories and their colourful heroines. It was on the return journey later that day that something happened to alter their alliance.

Anna Muller had left her spot in the park a little earlier that after-noon. She had missed her daily interaction with Eileen over the past few days and wanted to buy the young girl a few sweets to show her how much she had missed their conversations. And so when Eileen took her seat beside her companion a while later, she was greeted with a broad smile and a gift-wrapped box of toffees. Eileen was over-joyed, the packaging was so pretty with its yellow ribbon and printed card but most of all she was overwhelmed by the kindness of Mrs. Muller. These were no ordinary candies.

'Thank you so much', gushed Eileen, 'They're fabulous'.

'I hope you enjoy them dear child', replied Anna, 'I'm just so glad you're feeling better'.

'Oh yes, I am', came the response 'Better than ever'.

Mrs. Muller patted Eileen's hand, 'Good, I'm very glad'. But as the larger hand rested momentarily on the smaller one, the Russian couldn't help but notice how cold the girl's hands were.

'Dear me, where are your gloves?' she exclaimed. Eileen blushed, they were left behind in her desk.

'Here, borrow mine', offered Anna, and before the young girl could protest, a pair of soft red leather gloves were being thrust upon her.

'Wow, they're so glamorous!' Eileen enthused, 'You're like a model in the magazines Mrs. Muller!'

At that moment, Anna Muller lifted a cotton handkerchief to dab at a tear in the corner of her eye, she was overcome with emotion at the sweetness of this lovely golden-haired child. But in the same instance, Eileen happened to glance up at the sleek figure beside her and couldn't help but notice a row of crudely inked numbers tainting her delicate white wrist. Eileen knew at once what it was, both of her uncles had fought in the war and she had heard them talking in hushed tones about the atrocities in the German concentration camps. Could this wonderful, stylish lady really have been a prisoner in one of those places? Eileen's mind raced, she was hardly able to comprehend what she had seen.

The Russian pulled franticly at her sleeve, wanting to both cover the unsightly marks on her skin and to push them out of sight before this innocent child at her side could see. She already knew that it was too late.

Slowly, Anna Muller placed her hand on top of the young girl's and allowed the tears to fall freely down her cheeks, streaking her carefully applied make-up and causing her body to become rigid with grief. Now Eileen understood why this beautiful Russian needed the comfort and space that the outdoors afforded her. Her confinement had been a source of terror and continual ritual, forcing Anna to close doors within her mind to block out the dreadful memories of her years in captivity.

"It's okay Mrs. Muller", whispered Eileen, "I promise not to tell anyone."

"Thank you, it was such a terrible time in my life", replied Anna, "One I can never forget."

Eileen's mind raced. She had so many questions but knew that not one of them would leave her lips. Instead she sat silently contemplating the consequences of what she had just learned and felt a knot start to form in her stomach. There were now only two others passengers aboard the bus, but luckily they were deep in conversation and noticed none of the emotional turmoil unfolding in front of them. The driver had his eyes fixed firmly on the road, cautiously approaching corners just in case another vehicle was travelling the same road. High hedgerows and sharp bends made it a difficult route to drive, and he too was oblivious to the steady flow of tears and hushed voices behind him.

As the bus neared the village, so Anna Muller regained her composure. She still held tightly on to Eileen's hand but slowly released her grip as they drew up at the end of the cul-de-sac where they both lived. For the first time, Anna and Eileen walked together towards their respective homes, a mutual bond between them, nothing needing to be said but everything understood. At the Muller's gate, Eileen turned to say goodbye but her friend was already unlatching the gate and hurrying indoors. It was Olive's voice that pierced the silence, telling her daughter to hurry in before she caught a cold. Some things never change, thought Eileen, but then again other things will never be the same.

"You're awfully quiet this evening", Olive fussed as she placed a hand on Eileen's forehead during tea, "I do hope you're not coming down with a cold."

"I've got one too", snivelled Barbara, feigning sickness, "Can I have a day off school?"

"No you can't you little madam. There's nothing wrong with you. And anyway, I was talking to your sister. Eileen, you look as white as a sheet, are you alright?"

"I'm fine, Mum", replied her eldest daughter, "I've got homework to do", and with a final parting glance Eileen slid out from her seat at the table and made her way upstairs to her bedroom.

Eileen sat at the bedroom window for a full half hour before even attempting to grapple with the long division sums awaiting her attention. She gazed up at the dark clouds, thinking that they very much resembled people's emotions, sometimes calm and unmoving but at other times causing a storm from which the only release was shelter and comfort. Eileen felt that she had grown up that afternoon. A piece of her heart had melted away and the innocence of her youth had given way to the real tragedies going on in the world around her. So many people had suffered in the war, and damage had been done that could never be repaired, both mentally and physically. She pondered about the life that Anna Muller must have had before her capture, such a genteel and refined woman must surely have had a privileged childhood, maybe her parents were members of the Russian aristocracy? But surely if that were the case, they would have been able to seek passage to America or Canada before the Germans invaded? Eileen's mind raced, one scenario after another pushing their way in to her thoughts, but her foremost concern was how her beautiful friend had to relive her innermost horrors every day of her life, that was something that she could never fail to forget.

After clearing away the tea plates later that evening, Olive noticed a pair of fashionable red gloves lying on the top of the sideboard. They really were beauties, a softer pair she had never seen, let alone been able to afford. Better return them to their rightful owner, she thought, and Olive knew exactly who that person was, after all there had been talk amongst the women in the village about how much a pair of gloves like that would cost. She stroked the soft leather with her forefinger before taking off her floral apron and heading out in to the hallway.

As she tapped at the back door of the Muller's house, Olive could hear raised voices. This obviously was a bad time and she would have to call back in the morning, she knew exactly how it felt to be interrupted by visitors whilst a disagreement was in full swing. But as she hesitated on the doorstep for a moment, Olive heard a thud as something was smashed against the wall. She dearly hoped that quiet Mr. Muller wasn't trying to throw his weight around, he didn't look like a bully but nobody knew what occurred beyond the walls of her neighbour's property. She would just wait another minute to make sure everything was alright.

As Olive huddled against the Muller's porch to take respite from the bitter wind, the argument inside grew in intensity and a further clatter confirmed that things were indeed being hurled across the room. As the volume of the residents voices increased, Olive could clearly make out both Anna and Wolfgang shouting in what she concluded to be German. She really didn't want to pry, but having a basic knowledge of the language thanks to her brothers, Olive stood transfixed as she attempted to translate the kerfuffle inside.

It seemed that Anna Muller had shown something to someone today, something that her husband thought needed to be kept a secret? Was that the right word? Yes, a secret. Olive struggled to keep up with the flow of words as she listened to the dispute, but was thankful that German was obviously Anna's second language after Russian, as she spoke much more slowly and pronounced than her husband.

It was on that thought that Olive stopped. Why were they speaking German? Despite his name, the villagers had insisted that Wolfgang Muller was Polish...

Olive pressed her ear to the keyhole.

Anna Muller was upset about her time in prison? Really? And what was that other word? Olive tutted to herself in frustration, sometimes knowing half a language was worse than being totally oblivious, she thought. She was sure the woman had used the word 'Camp'. Hairs had started to rise on Olive's neck, she had already heard far too much but was unable to tear herself away without finding out more. She waited with baited breath as another item was flung across the room.

Suddenly the male voice broke down and wept. He kept saying sorry, over and over, sorry, so sorry. There was silence for a few moments and then the distinctive smash of plates being thrown.

'Sorry?' screamed Anna Muller. 'I only agreed to marry you so that you would save my sister. What did you do to the rest of my family?!'

"It was out of my control", came the faint reply, "There was nothing I could do. Please, Anastasia forgive me. We can be happy, if only you will forget about those days."

"I will never ever stop hating you, Wolfgang Muller", roared the woman, "You evil, evil man."

Outside footsteps scurried away down the path. Olive's eyes were as wide as saucers as she gently slipped back in to the comfort of her own home.

Chapter Three
Marilyn Roberts

On the south side of the village, next to the little Norman church, stood a whimsical thatched cottage with latticed windows and a solid oak door. Upon that door was a huge brass knocker, depicting two mermaids entwined in what could be interpreted as either an embrace or a struggle, depending on how you looked at it. The children of the village fantasized that a wicked witch lived beyond the threshold of that quaint little abode but, being almost the last property on the lane, they seldom ventured there to see. As it was, the resident there was neither wicked nor a witch but she did have an enormous black cat called Cecil.

Cecil was a born hunter and a creature of habit. He liked to spend his days lying in front of the warm kitchen stove in the winter or outside asleep under a rose bush in the summer. His evenings were filled with chasing anything that moved around the neat little graveyard next door and depositing his finds on the doorstep for his human companion to find in the morning. Little did the occupant of the cottage know but it was due to all the dead mice and bats lying on her doorstep each day that the local children had supposed something sinister was happening inside her cozy home. Every morning, as they rode the bus to school, the youngsters would press their faces up against the windows to see how many 'ingredients' the witch had collected for her pot the night before. And sure enough, they were never disappointed as a little bundle of dead vermin was always sure to sit proudly on the bristly mat outside.

The 'witch' carried on with her daily tasks, oblivious to the dark rumours about her, until the Easter after Olive and Geoff's arrival in the village.

As was customary in many parishes, the schoolchildren were given two weeks holiday in between their spring and summer terms. This was delightful for the youngsters but a difficult time for their parents, as it was a nightmare trying to keep them occupied at a time of year when rainstorms were plentiful and money to spend on extra outings was in short supply. Therefore every fine morning over Easter, the village children were sent out to discover their own entertainment, whether it be riding bicycles, picking wild flowers or helping the elderly members of the community with odd jobs in exchange for a few shillings. Olive's children were no exception but the two girls were as different as chalk and cheese. While Eileen would help her mother around the house, read books or take long bicycle rides with her friends, Barbara was a different matter entirely. Anything that could be discovered, deconstructed or totally demolished found its way into her path. Barbara liked to think of herself as naturally curious but unfortunately that wasn't the opinion of the parents whose children she goaded in to helping her with her devilish plans, they thought her rude, selfish and a thorn in her mother's side.

And so, with school over for a fortnight, her sister engrossed in cookery lessons with their mother, and the rest of the village children under strict instructions to behave themselves, Barbara had devised a plan to keep herself occupied for the duration of the break. She was going to visit the 'witch'.

Now Barbara was a fearless but very foolish girl and often acted on impulse without thinking through the possible consequences of her actions, and on that particular Monday morning she marched down the lane as fast as her legs would carry her but had no inkling as to what she would say or do once she had arrived at the 'witch's' door. It was a fairly breezy morning and Olive had insisted that her youngest daughter wear a red raincoat which was neither comfortable nor inconspicuous but served the intended purpose of keeping her warm and dry. Therefore as Barbara approached her destination, she couldn't help but feel a likeness to Little Red Riding Hood about to meet her nemesis.

Standing on the doormat with her hand raised to the odd mermaid knocker, Barbara paused. She really should have thought this through, thought up an excuse to be standing here and at least created a dialogue in her mind of what she was going to say. Sadly it was too late. As Barbara deliberated, the door opened with an eerie creak and a woman dressed in black stood in the doorway in front of her.

'Arghhhhhh', screamed Barbara, 'Arghhhhh'.

'What on earth is the matter...?' the woman started to ask, but it was too late, all she could see now was a little red raincoat retreating in to the distance with a mass of ginger curls blowing around its hood.

'How strange', the woman shrugged, and closed the door.

Five minutes later a breathless and terrified Barbara stood panting in her mother's kitchen, she was shaking from head to toe and her knee-high socks had slipped down to her ankles and now resembled scrunched up cotton balls. It took a few moments for Olive to calm her daughter down and find out the cause of her distress. Immediately the tale was told, Eileen creased up with laughter and called her sister a 'Scaredy Cat' while Olive tried to hide her smirks with the corner of her apron.

'Sit down Barbara', she said 'Don't you know that there are no such things as witches, whatever you think you have seen only exists in storybooks'.

Barbara shook her head defiantly 'Mother, it was a witch. I know I saw a witch'.

Olive sighed. The morning would now have to be spent apologising to yet another victim of Barbara's vivid imagination. Leaving Eileen to watch over baby Godfrey, Olive pulled on her sage green coat and left the house shaking her head in defeat.

As she hurried through the village, Olive cursed to herself. She sincerely hoped that Barbara hadn't scared some poor old woman half to death and that medical assistance would be more appropriate than any attempt at an apology. As she neared the church, the little thatched cottage came in to view and Olive sighed deeply. Here goes, she thought.

The heavy brass knocker only needed to be rapped once before the door was opened. Olive sucked in her breath.

Before her stood a short woman of average looks wearing nondescript dark clothing but certainly not a person that resembled anything like a witch. In fact, the person before her looked like a typical middle-aged spinster. Olive quickly explained the reason for calling and was immediately invited inside for a cup of tea. It seemed that this lady understood a childish prank when she saw one and insisted that Olive had no need to explain her daughter's actions. In fact, Barbara's scream had added some much needed drama to the woman's mundane morning.

"I actually thought it was quite funny", the lady quipped, "The sight of those golden ringlets bouncing up and down was priceless."

"Well, as I said, I'm very sorry that Barbara bothered you. She's very highly strung."

The woman invited Olive to sit in a chintz armchair next to the fire, where an enormous black cat lay sleeping, oblivious to the guest who was eying him with interest. While a pot of tea was prepared, Olive cast an appraising eye around the room. Everything seemed to be coordinated to perfection, with the mint green curtains and pale pink cushions complimenting the wild rose patterns of the wallpaper. There were clusters of family photographs dotted around the surfaces of highly polished furniture and a pretty collection of china plates perched precariously on a well-crafted Welsh dresser. As the two women chatted and ate slices of fruit cake, Olive noticed that there were very few lines around the other woman's eyes, she was perhaps only a few years older than Olive herself, but strangely she did have a few straggly grey hairs protruding from her chin. Olive tried not to stare but was fascinated as to the woman's age, no wrinkles but a hairy chin pointed towards poor genes in her estimation. It also occurred to Olive that the woman had an unusually gruff voice too. Perhaps she was recovering from a particularly bad cold poor love. Still, she made a good cup of tea and excellent cake, so perhaps the two could become friends after all.

An hour passed in amiable conversation. Olive learned that her new acquaintance was called Marilyn Roberts, which made her smile inwardly. It was an unusual combination of Hollywood glamour and English tradition but oddly it suited her. Marilyn had never been married, which Olive had guessed from the moment she clapped eyes on her, and she worked from home as a seamstress, taking in work from several boutiques and haberdashery stores in the town. Judging by the beautiful beaded gown that hung on a dummy in the corner of the room, Olive thought that Marilyn must be very good at her job.

"It's made from organza and chiffon", explained Marilyn proudly, "Takes me hours to sew on all those little pearls on by hand."

Olive nodded approvingly, it really was a wonderful piece of workmanship.

In turn, Olive imparted bits of her own family life, telling Marilyn about her caring husband, her very opposite girls and her precious baby boy. On the last topic, Olive was alerted to the fact that she had left Eileen caring for little Godfrey, who would be due for his feed any time now. Olive hurriedly put on her coat and said her goodbyes to her new friend. Marilyn was sad to see Olive go but invited her to call again soon. Olive said that she would and left the cottage on a high.

Geoffrey was intrigued to hear all about 'the Witch' that evening, and chuckled as his wife recounted how Barbara had scared herself silly that morning.

"That'll teach her", he laughed, "Maybe she'll keep out of mischief for a while now."

"I certainly hope so", replied Olive shaking her head, "She's such a handful."

"So what is this 'Witch' like then?" Geoff asked his youngest daughter as she looked at him sheepishly over her cup of warm milk.

"Scary, that's what", replied the red-headed minx, "I still think she's a witch."

Both parents laughed heartily. Maybe one of these days Barbara would learn a valuable lesson about keeping out of trouble, but she never ceased to provide them with a source of entertainment.

"She's actually a very nice lady", finished Olive, "She's got a gorgeous tomcat called Cecil."

"Oh, no you don't", started Geoff wagging his forefinger at his wife, "We've got enough mouths to feed in this house without bringing strays in to it."

Olive shrugged, this wouldn't be the first nor last time that the subject of a cat had been broached.

It wasn't until the two girls were back at school that Olive had chance to take baby Godfrey out for a stroll on her own, and as soon as she did, Olive headed down the lane to the little thatched cottage once again. She only intended to say a quick hello, after all she had left bread rising on the kitchen windowsill and there were numerous household chores which needed her attention. Olive looked down at Godfrey, who was busy examining a corner of his wool blanket.

"Shall we go and say good morning to Marilyn", she cooed, "Shall we?"

Godfrey squealed with delight and kicked his tiny toes wildly.

"Come on then", giggled Olive, tickling the bottom of his foot, "Let's see if the pussycat's there."

Marilyn was as welcoming as on the first occasion and busied herself with making refreshments whilst Olive settled Godfrey on the rug in front of her, where he chuckled and cooed at Cecil the cat. Cecil was most obliging and stretched his great body out in front of the infant, enticing him to stroke the fur on his huge black underside.

A brand new Singer sewing machine was set up on a lace-covered table in one corner, and the hem of a velvet jacket lay neatly clamped underneath its needle.

"I didn't mean to interrupt you if you're busy…" ventured Olive, "If you need to get this finished…"

"Don't be silly", enthused her friend, "I'm due a break anyway, I'll just finish that seam."

Olive watched admiringly as the spinster deftly cranked the handle of the machine with her right hand, while guiding the fabric carefully along with her left. Less than a minute later, the two ends of the cotton had been tied and the finished item hung loosely on a wooden hanger.

"I'm so happy that you came", enthused Marilyn, "I rarely get visitors and it can be so lonely with only that big furry devil for company."

Olive glanced down at Cecil, "He's lovely, I sometimes think that we should get a cat."

"Oh do", replied her friend, sitting down in the opposite armchair, "They're wonderful pets."

Olive noticed that Marilyn was looking slightly more glamorous than on her first visit. She couldn't quite decide whether it was the addition of a touch of rouge or the way that the other woman had pulled her hair up into a high chignon, but she definitely looked better for it. On closer inspection, but very discreetly of course, Olive wondered whether her new friend was in fact wearing a wig. There was something a little too perfect about the smooth hairstyle that Marilyn now sported and the colour of the hair was so very different to the last time she had visited. Still, one couldn't chide a woman for wanting to take care of herself and the glamorous spinster was certainly doing just that. Ever the matchmaker, Olive wondered whether her bachelor brother would be interested in taking Marilyn out on a date. Although she didn't have the usual style or pretty face that her sibling looked for in a woman, Marilyn was polite, self-sufficient and mild-mannered. Olive thought it a genuine possibility.

"I'll make us a drink", the woman called as she disappeared along the hallway and in to the kitchen, "Make yourself at home. Give your little lad one of those bananas in the fruit bowl."

Olive looked around. Not a speck of dust to be seen anywhere, it was good to meet someone as house proud as herself. She glanced toward the sideboard, where the framed pictures that she remembered from her first visit stood lined up along the polished surface. One in particular caught her eye. A young boy of around four or five years old sat in a wicker chair with his arms folded. A frown wrinkled his brow and the corners of his lips were turned downwards as if he were very cross indeed about something. Olive smirked, she had plenty of pictures of Barbara with that exact same expression. Children, who could predict their moods?

Behind her, Marilyn entered the room and set down a heavily laden wooden tray.

"Oh, I see you've noticed the family photos", she laughed, "He was a little tyke that one."

"A nephew?' Olive asked innocently, expecting Marilyn to elaborate.

"No", came the unexpected answer, "Just someone I used to know."

Olive didn't like to pry further, she had a good instinct for when someone had opened up as much as they were going to, so she turned away from the pictures and busied herself pouring tea.

As they chatted over refreshments and watched Godfrey play with Cecil the cat, Olive and Marilyn found they had more than a few things in common. They both had a passion for cooking, came from large families, loved fashion and both had a secret penchant for handbags. As they discovered this last bond, Marilyn stood up and opened a large built-in cupboard next to the fireplace. Olive's eyes widened as she feasted her eyes on more handbags than she could count. They were neatly lined up in order of colour, with the white ones on the top shelf, passing through peaches, reds, blues and purples, until finally on the very bottom shelf stood a row of black patent delights, standing upright like a black-painted picket fence.

'Oh my goodness', gasped Olive, 'How wonderful. This is my idea of handbag heaven."

'My substitute for a husband and children', smiled Marilyn, 'But don't tell the vicar!'

Olive laughed, how marvelous to have discovered a woman with such a wonderful obsession. She was sure the two of them would become great friends. Her own great passion was hats, but every outfit needed a matching handbag and it seemed that Marilyn had every possible colour co-ordination covered with this fabulous collection. She smiled and scanned the shelf once more, pure handbag heaven!

"You're more than welcome to borrow one any time you like", offered Marilyn unexpectedly, "You only have to say the word."

"Oh, that's very kind", gasped Olive, genuinely overwhelmed, "But I'm not sure that I go anywhere posh enough to warrant using one of those!"

"Well, the offer's there. Any time you like."

Olive smiled warmly at her friend. She was beginning to feel very comfortable in Marilyn's company.

Godfrey's niggling brought the two ladies back to reality and Olive suddenly realised that she had been sitting in Marilyn's home for over two hours. It was time to get back to her own house, where laundry, dusting and the evening meal were all waiting to be seen to. And the bread, thought Olive, by now it would have risen to the top of the mixing bowl! As she bid farewell, Olive gave Marilyn a little squeeze on the arm and invited her new friend to call round any time, but the invite was received with hesitance and excuses. Marilyn didn't venture far from home apparently, especially not to that end of the village, but Olive was more than welcome to come again she said, in fact Marilyn insisted.

Olive's visits to Marilyn's little cottage became a regular occurrence with both women enjoying the other's company immensely. They had no end to chat about and often traded favours too, with Marilyn offering to make new summer dresses for the girls and Olive providing her friend with a crocheted throw for her bed and any batches of jam that she happened to be making that week.

Olive was always careful to spend no more than an hour at the cottage, as she was aware how easy it was to get behind with her household chores. Marilyn was always busy too, working on some new ball gown or another but she always seemed happy to put her sewing aside to spend some time chatting. It had been a cold spring but thankfully summer came early, giving the two ladies plenty of opportunities to take their pot of tea outdoors and relax in the warm sunshine. Cecil the cat was always around somewhere, either hiding in the bushes or stretched out on a window ledge, and it soon became a game for Godfrey to seek him out and tickle the feline's big furry tummy.

On one particular visit, Olive noticed that Marilyn wasn't her usual chatty self.

"You seem a bit down today, love", clucked Olive, "Is everything alright?"

'Oh, I'm okay", her friend replied, but with a saddened tone in her voice, "It's just I've heard that my mother's not well and I'm not sure whether I should visit."

Olive coaxed the other woman to explain the reason for her reluctance to take the short bus ride to her mother's village only a few miles away. It seemed that they were no longer close, but what had happened to cause the rift was something that Marilyn seemed to want to keep to herself. Still, Olive could see the pain in her friend's eyes and assured her that, no matter what had happened, family was the most important thing in a person's life. A visit would do Marilyn the world of good.

"I know you mean well dear", said Marilyn as she cleared away the tea cups that afternoon, "It's just been such a very long time."

Olive patted her friend's hand and turned to leave, "At least think about it, eh?"

The next time Olive called on her new friend was after Church service one Sunday. Geoffrey had offered to take all three children to his parents for the afternoon as he could see that Olive had 'one of her headaches' (which incidentally usually occurred at the mere mention of Geoffrey's parents) and needed some peace and quiet. It was always a source of amusement to Olive when she attended Church without her family. A soft murmur could faintly be heard as she took her usual seat beside the vicar's wife, and occasionally the voices rose in volume to confirm her suspicions that the rest of the congregation thought her and Geoff had quarreled, hence the noticeable absence of her loved ones. Of course, nobody ever directly asked Olive the reason for her husband's nonappearance, and neither did she offer any explanation. It was rather fun to leave them guessing, she thought.

As the parishioners stood to sing the first hymn, their leather-bound books open at the relevant page, Olive glanced across the aisle to where the Mullers were standing rigidly side by side. Anna Muller looked as resplendent as usual in a smart camel-coloured coat, her soft lips forming every word of the song perfectly, while her bespectacled husband kept his head high and his back stiff, as though standing to attention in an army parade. Apart from Geoff, she had told no-one about the strange conversation that she had heard outside their house those few months ago. Besides, what if she had interpreted the conversation incorrectly? Although she was positive that she hadn't. And what would people think when they realised that to have discovered such a dark secret, Olive must have been listening at other people's keyholes! That in itself would be enough to keep the gossip-mongers fueled for weeks! She shuffled her feet to keep them warm and stole another furtive glance towards Anna Muller. The tall Russian caught her eye and smiled politely. Olive flushed but managed to keep enough composure to conceal her inner thoughts from being revealed. Poor woman, Olive reflected, fancy having to carry those awful memories with you, and as for her fiend of a husband, why had he never been taken to trial for his diabolical actions? She shuddered, both from the draughts that seeped through the church doors and from the sudden realisation that she would never be able to tell another living soul about her dreadful discovery.

Worship continued and Olive was soon absorbed in the reading being delivered by the tiny mouse-like shopkeeper, Elsie Corbett. It had been a lovely service with Reverend Todd giving a sermon on helping thy neighbour in need. As she waited in line to shake the pastor's hand, Olive reflected upon the words that had been spoken in his lecture. She had seen the folk around her nodding approvingly, clearly full of their own intentions to lend someone a hand, visit the sick or write a long overdue letter to a distant relative. Olive doubted whether anyone in her cul-de-sac were in particular need of anything, therefore she settled on visiting Marilyn who might need a bit of company if nothing else.

The cottage garden was immaculate as usual and Olive could see that her friend was obviously at home, as she observed a thin wisp of smoke winding its way up to the sky from the chimney-pot ahead. Cecil was stretched out on the doormat and raised his head sleepily as Olive gently stroked the back of his ears. She tugged at the heavy brass knocker, once again wondering where on earth Marilyn had found such a strange object. There was a faint shuffling sound from inside but nobody came to answer the door. The distinctive sound of footsteps upon a tiled floor could be heard very faintly, as if they came from the back of the house. Olive looked back down at Cecil, who was now fully awake and anticipating the opening of the door in case there was a chance of being fed. She shrugged at the wide-eyed feline, waited a few moments and knocked again, this time a little harder in case the first rap had gone unheard.

After another short period of odd noises, a rather flushed Marilyn opened the door. Her pale pink cardigan was buttoned up incorrectly, revealing a cream coloured lace camisole underneath and her hair looked slightly disheveled. Marilyn appeared to be panting somewhat, causing the other woman to conclude that she had been caught in a predicament and had dressed pretty hastily. Olive felt awkward, obviously she had called at an inconvenient time, the other woman hadn't even put her stockings on and thick dark stubble covered the bottom half of her legs! For one embarrassing moment Olive wondered if Marilyn had company, and perhaps if that 'company' were male. That would explain the red cheeks and half-dressed appearance of her friend. There was an awkward silence for a few seconds, neither woman not quite knowing what to say.

'I'm so sorry, I shouldn't have called unexpectedly', muttered Olive, 'I'll be on my way'.

Marilyn started to say something but stopped, maybe it was better if she didn't try to explain.

'Good bye', said Olive as she retreated up the path, 'I'll see you another time'.

With that, Olive hastily unlatched the wooden gate and made her way back past the church where several stragglers were still saying their goodbyes to the vicar. She was aware that she probably looked quite flustered but Olive was in no mind to stop and offer an explanation, so marched back up the lane as if on a mission until she reached her own back door. Only then did Olive compose her thoughts and begin to wonder whether she had over-reacted. After all, Marilyn was fully entitled to have male visitors should she wish to do so, perhaps it was just the shock of potential Sunday afternoon frolicking that had got Olive so hot under the collar?

Far behind, Marilyn stood in her own doorway saying nothing but feeling ridiculous as her friend scuttled away, there was nothing to hide, she had only been taking a nap. No Casanova lay spread-eagled on the eiderdown waiting to cover her body in kisses, she was simply taking a nap. Something would have to be done to recover her reputation. It didn't matter what the rest of the village thought she got up to behind closed doors, but Olive, she was a very good friend, the kind that were worth keeping.

Olive arrived home to the silence of an empty house, and exchanged her patent shoes for a pair of soft sheepskin slippers. She flicked on the radio and began filling the kettle to make herself some tea, but stopped when she realised that she had run out of sugar. Damn it! Was everything going to be a disaster today? Be a good Samaritan, love thy neighbour, so much for that! she huffed. Olive's thoughts were still back at the little cottage. She tutted at herself for over-reacting at her friend's unexpectedly bedraggled appearance, good luck to her if she had managed to find a man at long last! Wasn't that exactly what Marilyn needed? Someone to love and cherish her? I should be the last person to judge, she told herself defiantly, there are plenty of others who are willing to do that!

An hour later Marilyn stood on Olive's doorstep, red leather bag in hand and a black pillbox hat covering the crown of her platinum and grey streaked hair. I really shouldn't have come, Marilyn told herself. She could already see a couple of the villagers craning their necks to see who the lady was that had passed by their windows and before long the whole community would be out in force to have a good look.

Why wasn't Olive answering the door? Was she ignoring her friend because of what she'd seen? Maybe she's upstairs, the woman thought, I'll just give it a few minutes more.

As Marilyn stood knocking at her friend's door, Olive was in fact two doors away borrowing sugar from her neighbour, Mrs. Hargreaves. As the local store was closed on Sundays, it was quite common for the villagers to 'borrow' supplies from one another, concluding the transaction over a cup of tea. Such a scenario was now taking place, with Mrs. Hargreaves setting two China cups and saucers down on the table in front of her and Olive.

'There we go dear", clucked Mrs. Hargreaves, "Can't beat a good brew can you?"

Olive nodded eagerly in agreement. "Especially when someone else makes it for you."

Both women chuckled. Just what I needed, mused Olive, I feel better already.

Mrs. Hargreaves was quite the opposite of most of the women that Olive had already encountered in the village. Loud and brash with crooked teeth, she smoked rolling tobacco and dyed her hair with henna. Olive didn't' mind that the other woman asked a lot of questions and was always angling for gossip, in fact she found it quite amusing that her neighbours were all so very different. She would never have imagined the Hargreaves' being together but they seemed happy enough. Polar opposites in both looks and personalities, the couple were complete misfits. But, I have to hand it to them, admitted Olive, they have two of the most polite children in the village.

Mrs. Hargreaves bustled about searching the cupboards for biscuits whilst simultaneously rubbing a trail of cigarette ash in to the rug with her stockinged feet.

They were just taking their first sips when the door connecting the kitchen to the lounge was abruptly opened by Mr. Hargreaves, who reeled in to the kitchen with tears rolling down his cheeks. He was shirtless and wore a string vest under red braces, which served to hold up a huge pair of tweed trousers, over an even huger stomach. His feet were covered in tartan slippers and he carried the sports section of a national newspaper in his hand.

Both women looked up startled.

'Whatever is the matter with you Stan?' demanded Mrs. Hargreaves.

Her husband held his sides and hooted loudly 'It's Martin, outside Olive's', he gasped.

'Martin who?' queried Olive, looking puzzled. But Stan Hargreaves was in no condition to explain and continued to laugh uncontrollably. His face had now become so flushed that he gasped for breath and began fanning himself with the newspaper. A long bead of sweat ran slowly down one side of his face and a globule of spittle had gathered at the side of his mouth.

Both women rose from their seats at the table and peered through the kitchen window. Olive was just in time to see Marilyn making a hasty retreat back towards the main thoroughfare but there was certainly no gentleman called Martin accompanying her.

'God Lord', exclaimed Mrs. Hargreaves 'He hasn't been up here for years'.

'Who?' asked Olive, now beginning to get very frustrated that nothing was being explained to her.

'Martin Roberts', replied her neighbour, shaking her head sadly as if someone had died.

'I can only see my friend Marilyn', said Olive, craning her neck in case another person was out of view.

'Oh dear', said Mrs. Hargreaves, now taking Olive by the elbow and leading her back to the kitchen chair, 'I think you might need a drop of brandy in your tea dear'.

'Brandy in my tea? Will somebody please tell me what's going on!' demanded Olive.

Stan Hargreaves finally stopped laughing and turned to face his visitor. He slapped a big chunky palm on his thigh and let out a deep breath.

'There is no Marilyn', he said 'Only Martin, in ladies clothes', upon which he started chuckling again.

Chapter Four
Reverend Todd

Olive had been going to church in the village for some time now and had come to think of her attendance as second nature. Not a Sunday went past when she didn't dress up in one of her pretty frocks, polish her best shoes and occasionally leave instructions with Geoff on what time to put the meat into the oven for roasting. On three out of four Sundays, Geoff would join his wife just to appease her, but he had little religious inclination himself, preferring to believe in fate rather than some higher being. Besides it being her main weekly social event, Olive also enjoyed the time away from her family responsibilities and looked forward to the ten minutes or so of pleasant chatter with her fellow church-goers afterwards. With both of her girls at Sunday school for the duration of the service and little Godfrey settled in his pram while his father tinkered in the garage, Olive could fully relax, reflect on the week behind her and give thanks for all the wonderful things that the good Lord had bestowed upon her.

The fact that the church was in full view of Marilyn, or perhaps Martin Roberts' cottage and vice versa, was a slight embarrassment to Olive. She hadn't quite recovered from the shock of learning that she had frequently been sharing afternoon tea with a man. Geoff had ribbed her about it for days afterwards but, keen to exonerate herself, Olive had been quick to point out that Geoff hadn't noticed the fact that her friend was a cross-dresser either. On the rare occasion that Olive did catch a glimpse of someone in the cottage garden she would raise her hand in a quick wave, then hurry on her way. She had been too shocked to go and speak to the man, after all she felt deceived, but Olive bore no hard feelings, and instead missed their afternoons of laughter. And so, it was with a heavy heart that she strolled through the graveyard to meet her fellow parishioners.

Reverend Todd was a wonderful vicar. He always seemed to choose a topic for his sermon that was either close to Olive's heart or relevant to some incident that had happened recently in the village and with which she could connect personally. On their way out of church at the end of service, the entire congregation would shuffle slowly out through the huge arched doorway as the person in front of them paused to shake hands with Reverend Todd and thank him for yet another thought-provoking service. Olive was definitely not alone in her admiration for the Parish priest, as each and every villager would be full of compliments from the choice of hymns to the Reverend's compassion for the sick and elderly.

It also did no harm to the vicar's female follower's that he was also charming and handsome, with only slightly greying hair at his temples giving away a hint of his true age. The ladies of the village hung on to the clergyman's every word and Olive was no exception. It was such a refreshing change to meet a vicar with modern ideas, instead of the stuffy old relics who had conducted the repetitive services in the villages of Olive's youth. She remembered many a Sunday morning being gently pinched by her mother as she fell in to a light doze, head nodding gently as the preacher in the pulpit scorned the Devil and urged the parishioners to confess their sins before emptying the coins in their pockets on to the enormous collection plate being handed around. Wasn't it funny, she had asked her mother, how churches were always in need of funds for repair? Olive's mother had laughed and said something about money for the elderly priest's drinking habits too. It wasn't until now, with the wisdom that can only come with maturity, that Olive fully appreciated that comment and it still made her smile.

Mrs. Todd was revered just as much as her husband in the community. She had taken on the responsibility of teaching Sunday school in the village hall, organised fetes and whist drives, and visited those in need of company and a sympathetic ear. Olive always thought that Mrs. Todd fitted the stereo-typical mould of a vicar's wife to perfection. She never dressed too ostentatiously, preferring twin-set and pearls to any garishly printed dresses, and wore her long dark hair neatly in a bun which show-cased her smooth complexion and make-up free skin. Despite the villagers always being encouraged to call her Cynthia, a name that both suited her and was easy to remember, most people called the Reverend's wife by her married title which was both a mark of respect to her husband's status and a way of showing how much they appreciated her singular efforts at fund-raising and boosting community morale. Mrs. Todd was certainly very easy to get along with and seemed just as amiable with the senior citizens in the parish as with the children to whom she imparted Bible classes. Olive was certainly very impressed with the way in which her own two daughters showed enthusiasm for their Sunday school lessons and Barbara, who was very often stubborn when it came to tuition, had even been heard singing hymns in the bath.

The vicarage was quite a grand but slightly run-down house which stood in immaculate gardens directly opposite the church. Although not modern by today's standards, it was built far more recently than most of the other village dwellings and stood out as such, with its perfectly square windows and red brick exterior. It was quite a large place for just three occupants, the third being the Todd's pretty young daughter Caroline, but they seemed content enough with their lot and went to great lengths to ensure that their door was always open should any parishioner feel the need to drop by.

As with most rural communities, significant religious and seasonal festivals were always a time for the villagers to pull together in an effort to show their support to both their local church and to each other. Harvest Festival was one such occasion and for weeks before the main event of distributing hampers to the elderly and adorning the church interior with wheat sheaves and flowers, the women of the village would hold numerous meetings to delegate tasks and to work out schedules for polishing the large amount of wood and brass that needed constant upkeep.

Olive was only too happy to volunteer her services, and was delighted when she was included in the pre-Harvest Festival meetings held at the vicarage each Monday evening for a month beforehand. She hadn't really known what to expect when she had eagerly signed up to join the other women in their duties, but was happy just to be a part of the gatherings and was willing to undertake any given task. At the first meeting, Olive had nervously knocked at the vicarage door, wondering exactly what the women would be talking about and how formal these discussions were. If there was ever a moment of doubt about her acceptance in to the group, it was banished from Olive's mind within thirty seconds of stepping in to the magnolia hallway. Reverend Todd greeted her with a wide pearly-white smile, took her coat and scarf, and then ushered Olive in to the large and comfortable sitting room where nine other women chatted informally over cups of steaming Earl Grey tea.

The vicarage sitting room was high-ceilinged and spacious, with oil paintings depicting country scenes adorning the walls and heavy drapes hanging across both of the south-facing windows. Olive couldn't help but notice the abundance of newspapers and periodicals that had been crammed in to the magazine rack, and the groaning bookshelves holding everything from 19th century poetry to a teach yourself book on watercolours. It was exactly how she had imagined it would be, homely, large and comfortable.

In the centre of the room stood Mrs. Todd, smiling at the ladies around her and holding a huge catering sized teapot which she now held out towards her new guest. Olive gratefully picked up a clean china cup and saucer from the sideboard and allowed her host to fill it to the brim. A couple of buxom ladies now quickly shuffled together on the sofa, making room for Olive to sit down and join the lively conversation. With cups replenished and biscuits handed around, Reverend Todd cleared his throat and the meeting began.

'My dear ladies", he began, "Let me first thank you all for coming. Without you, our Harvest Festival celebrations would not be possible. Each and every one of you are absolute angels."

There was a murmur of consent as the women absorbed the compliment and then each item on the agenda was carefully addressed with actions and delegates quickly being decided.

It seemed to Olive that the Reverend and Mrs. Todd were used to conducting discussions full of constant interruption and intermittent laughter, but the ladies in attendance meant no disrespect, they were simply excited at the prospect of being a part of the upcoming event. For over an hour the agenda was perused and agreed, with Olive volunteering to help with the colossal task of cleaning the church artifacts, aided by her neighbour Mrs. Hargreaves. With headway made, more tea was offered and the conversation took a more general turn, with several of the women now complimenting Mrs. Todd on her beautiful home and exquisite taste in tea. Olive was starting to feel a real sense of camaraderie with the other ladies and soon found herself chatting about her children and the district from which she and Geoff had moved the year before. Each new piece of information was accepted with a smile, a courteous nod or a murmur of approval, and Olive enjoyed the attention a great deal.

The next meeting followed pretty much the same format, with cups of tea and platefuls of biscuits being consumed before getting down to business. The women seemed to be sitting in exactly the same seats as on the previous occasion, which caused Olive to smirk slightly as she made her way over to her place on the sofa. The rigid ways of these country folk never ceased to be a source of amusement to her, even Geoff had started to comment on how the same people caught the bus to town every Saturday morning and that the men of the village always appeared at the same time every Sunday to mow their lawns and trim their hedges.

"Everything okay Olive? You seem miles away?'

Olive lifted her gaze to where Reverend Todd stood looking down at her.

"I'm fine thank you, just wondering which Harvest Festival task I'm best suited for."

The vicar smiled and patted her shoulder gently, "

"A talented young lady such as yourself would be an asset to us in any capacity."

Olive blushed and took another sip of tea. She had never met such a charming man of the cloth before, he certainly had a way of chatting to the ladies. Her thoughts were soon interrupted by the sound of Mrs. Todd coughing loudly in an attempt to get the meeting underway. She wore yet another jumper and cardigan combination, this time in powder blue, and had carefully selected a thin belt for her skirt in the same hues. Olive would never cease to be amazed at the pride in their appearance that these villagers took. It was like a never-ending fashion parade! Still, Olive was a great lover of clothes and looked forward to Geoff giving her the weekly housekeeping money, from which she would save a few shillings in order to buy new outfits for herself and the children but she also enjoyed comparing fashion and beauty tips with the ladies of the village too, and she now glanced around the room to see which women were sporting a new hairstyle or shade of lipstick. Such an amiable group, she thought, and I'm delighted to be a part of their community.

The following weekend, Olive found herself in the company of Mrs. Hargreaves as they walked briskly towards the church with one basket full of brass cleaning fluid and cotton rags, with which they intended to fulfill their nominated task and another containing refreshments for their lunch. Olive couldn't help but think her neighbour was a rather over-dressed for the task at hand, with her fashionable mauve dress and cream patent shoes, but she made no comment. A wide patent belt cinched in Mrs. Hargreaves' waist, which only caused more emphasis on her ample bosom and shapely behind. Her own choice of clothing had been much more practical and Olive sported a light cotton blouse, loose fitting trousers and a pair of flat leather pumps. She would have the last laugh later on, as Mrs. Hargreaves was bound to complain about her sore feet and stained attire. It never ceased to amaze Olive, the lengths that some women would go to for the sake of fashion.

It was a warm and sunny morning, and both women were in good spirits considering the arduous task that lay ahead of them that day. They chatted happily as they left their homes behind and stopped for a few minutes to say good morning to Peter Bristow who was already half way through mowing the grass in the cemetery. Peter was a cheerful fellow and his obvious devotion to keeping the grounds looking neat ensured that the little church looked in pristine condition. Olive looked around admiringly. This was certainly what life in a close-knit community was all about, everyone pulling together and helping to maintain the very heart of the village.

'Morning, ladies" Peter bellowed over the top of the buzzing machine, "Lovely day for it."

Olive and Mrs. Hargreaves nodded in agreement.

"He's a cheerful soul", enthused Olive's companion, "Always got a smile on his face."

"He certainly seems like a very decent sort" she replied, smiling.

The huge oak door was unlocked as usual, even at this early hour, as such peaceful community churches had no need to have their doors secured against thieves in these tranquil little parishes. Mrs. Hargreaves took Olive's basket from her and gently placed it on a pew in the front row. On their journey down the lane, the two women had decided it would be most productive if one started at the rear of the church, polishing candlesticks and the collection plate, while the other began cleaning the numerous decorative crosses on top of the altar, that way they could meet in the middle to share their flasks of tea and parcels of sandwiches half way through the day.

As she began her work at the altar, aided by the beams of sunlight which now shone through the elegant stained glass windows, Olive marveled at how just being inside a house of God could humble a person. She felt as though the Lord were constantly watching over his flock with tender care, and now looked down upon the two women as they started their menial tasks with vigour and diligence. The eerie lack of noise added a theatrical quality to the inside of building too, with the only audible sounds being soft thuds as the two ladies moved around in companionable silence.

After an hour of rubbing and polishing, there was a loud click as the door was opened and Reverend Todd stepped inside. He greeted the women with his usual warmth and gratitude, complimenting them both on their work with the brasses and thanking them again for taking time away from their busy households to assist with the necessary duties in the church. Olive wondered how the vicar always managed to give the aura of a movie star, with his silky soft voice and handsome good looks.

'I was wondering if you ladies would like to join me for lunch at the vicarage today,' the Reverend asked 'I'd be grateful for the company, as my wife has taken Caroline in to town to buy new shoes'.

Mrs. Hargreaves shot a glance in Olive's direction, they had already decided to stop for minimal time to eat their packed-lunches today, as both wanted to return home in order to relax for an hour before preparing tea for their families. Olive gave a little shrug. It would be impolite not to accept the vicar's offer, especially if he needed some company. Mrs. Hargreaves mimicked her friend's gesture and told the Reverend that they would be happy to join him, providing he agreed to share the food which they had already prepared.

'Excellent', nodded the vicar, smiling even more eagerly than usual, 'But I do insist that I make us all a nice pot of tea and throw in some of my wife's delicious Bakewell tart. Shall we say one o'clock?'

'One o'clock it is', replied Mrs. Hargreaves, "We'll be there, don't you worry about that."

A while later, with admirable progress underway and a great many brass objects now gleaming in the sunlight, Olive was more than ready to stop for lunch, as was her neighbour and they now headed outside to rinse their grubby hands under the water pump. As Mrs. Hargreaves stooped to splash water over her arms, Olive couldn't help but smile to herself. There were tell-tale signs of the morning's work on the other lady's frock and she didn't look quite so prim and proper any more. Maybe next time she would think twice before wearing her poshest dress to clean brasses! Anyway, each to their own, Olive thought, but she still felt justified in her decision to dress in a more appropriate manner.

It had been a long morning, with just one short break to drink tea and now both women could feel their stomachs rumbling in anticipation of their lunch at the vicarage.

It was the first time that Olive had set foot inside the Reverend's kitchen and she cast an appraising eye over the eclectic display of china plates that adorned a huge Welsh dresser and the sparkling white Belfast sink that was so clean it looked as though it had never been used. Mrs. Hargreaves had already made herself at home it seemed and she rested her bottom on the steel rail of the huge Aga stove, whilst smiling the whole time at the flustered vicar. Olive wondered whether her neighbour was a frequent visitor to the Todd's home. Something in the way that Mrs. Hargreaves casually leaned upon the fixtures and seemed to instinctively know where everything was kept told Olive that she probably was. Perhaps her and Cynthia Todd were good friends, she mused, although they hadn't exchanged much more than a few pleasantries at the Harvest Festival meeting. Oh well, Olive thought, I'm the newcomer around here, the other villagers have more than likely been close friends for years.

Reverend Todd had gone to great lengths to make his guests feel welcome and, besides the pot of tea, had laid a red gingham tablecloth over the huge kitchen table and set out plates and cups with fresh linen napkins folded neatly at the side of each place setting. The radio was on in the background, and as Olive and Mrs. Hargreaves were ushered to their seats, the latest American tunes now deftly mingled with the sound of the kettle whistling and a gentle splashing as the Reverend poured milk in to a jug.

Olive carefully started to unwrap the sandwiches which had lain in her basket all morning and said a silent thank you for the cold temperature inside the church which had helped to retain the freshness of their lunch. Mrs. Hargreaves wasn't known for her culinary skills and had left the sandwich-making to Olive, instead offering to provide the flasks of tea and some plums from her garden. Olive had been happy to oblige and had carefully prepared home-baked bread with two delicious fillings, ham and tomato and cheese with her brother's fabulous piccalilli. The trio tucked in without delay and soon finished their meal with a great deal of satisfaction. The conversation flowed easily, although Olive couldn't help but feel that her two companions were not taking a great deal of interest in what she had to say. Still, it had been a long morning and there was plenty of work to finish over the next couple of hours.

Being such conscientious ladies, it was quickly decided that Mrs. Hargreaves would stay to help the vicar clear away the crockery whilst Olive returned to her duties at the church. There were only a few plates and cups to wash up and Olive surmised that the unexpected lunchtime gathering would do little to disrupt their cleaning schedule.

"Thank you so much vicar", she babbled as they said their goodbyes, "It was so very kind of you."

"Not at all my dear", Reverend Todd answered, his perfect teeth glowing as he smiled at Olive.

"And don't take too long over those plates", she called jokingly back towards the kitchen where the other woman stood running warm water in to the sink.

"Right behind you Olive", yelled Mrs. Hargreaves, "I'll be ten minutes tops."

However, as it happened, it was an hour and a half later that Mrs. Hargreaves re-entered the church.

Feeling somewhat annoyed that her neighbour had very probably been partaking of more tea and Bakewell tart with Reverend Todd, Olive didn't look up from her task at hand, and therefore failed to notice the flushed face and tear-stained cheeks of the other woman. In fact, some minutes passed before she noticed the quiet snuffling and creaking woodwork as Mrs. Hargreaves sank down on to a wooden pew and began to search in her pockets for a clean handkerchief.

'Whatever's the matter?', asked Olive, trying to suppress the alarm in her voice as she dropped her blackened rags to the ground and made her way up the cold stone floor of the central aisle.

At first the other woman only hunched herself over and blew her nose noisily, ignoring the concern in Olive's voice and concentrating only on clearing her nasal passages. It wasn't until Olive took a seat next to her that Mrs. Hargreaves looked up and offered an explanation.

'Reverend Todd', she said in a whisper 'Has behaved in a very in-appropriate way."

"What, you mean he tried to...?" gasped Olive, suddenly realising what she was being told.

Mrs. Hargreaves nodded and burst in to tears again.

'Are you sure?' asked Olive, trying to keep her disbelief under control 'He's a man of the cloth!"

"Oh, yes, I'm sure. He's a wicked man, I feel so ashamed."

As Mrs. Hargreaves recounted the incident in detail, Olive's mind raced. It was hard to imagine. If what her friend was telling her about the clergyman was really true, they would have to report him, and she had no reason not to believe her neighbour. The woman at her side was certainly very distressed and the red rims around her eyes proved that she had obviously been crying for quite some time before returning to the church. Oh my goodness, their vicar was some kind of sex fiend!

'I don't want you to tell anyone about this', Mrs. Hargreaves sud-denly said, straightening her clothes and wiping away the last tear from her eye, 'My husband would be mortified'.

For the next ten minutes, Olive tried to make her friend see rea-son. Surely Reverend Todd should be held accountable for his actions, reported to the police, or reported to the Bishop.....

Despite her friend's concern and advice, Mrs. Hargreaves still in-sisted that the matter be kept between the two of them and made Olive promise that she would tell no-one about what had taken place at the vicarage that afternoon. Olive reluctantly agreed and wandered outside to fetch her companion a cup of water. Peter Bristow was pulling up weeds within a few yards of the water pump and turned when he heard the gravel crunch under Olive's feet.

"Everything alright, love?" he called, scrambling to his feet, "You look as white as a sheet."

Olive bit her lip and nodded. "I'm fine, thanks Peter. It's just getting a bit cold in there."

"Ay well, don't catch your death for the vicar" he chuckled, "He'll need you two ladies to help make the altar look impressive for Harvest Festival." With that, Peter Bristow turned back to pulling thistles up from the side of an ancient grave.

"No, we erm, we'll be going soon", faltered Olive, "I must get back and finish up."

With that, she rushed back through the main door, forgetting all about the water and feeling quite relieved that the man hadn't questioned her further. Olive's neighbour sat in the same position at the rear of the church, perfectly still and even more solemn than when she had returned from the vicarage. There was little that could be said to relieve the tension in the air and with no course of action seeming the right one, the two ladies sat in silence for several minutes. Neither woman felt that they could continue their brass cleaning duties and Olive insisted on clearing away the materials while Mrs. Hargreaves made her way home.

'Go and put your feet up, love" enthused Olive, rubbing her friend's arm, "And have a think."

Mrs. Hargreaves looked alarmed, her eyes widening like a rabbit caught in bright headlights.

"What about?"

"Well about what you're going to do of course!" gasped Olive, flabbergasted at the very idea that her neighbour was going to leave the matter unreported.

"Maybe", came the mumbled response, so quietly that the words could hardly be heard.

"It is a very serious matter", chided Olive, "What if he tries it on with someone else?"

The question went unheard, as Mrs. Hargreaves had already collected her belongings and was now scuttling out of the church, her heels clattering on the red tiled floor. Oh dear, she really ought to have thought things through and at least given some consideration to her rumpled clothing and tear-stained face before going back to her own home, reflected Olive. Goodness only knows what conclusions Stan Hargreaves might jump to seeing his wife turn up on the doorstep with a dirty dress and red eyes.

It didn't take long for Olive to gather up the polish and rags, but a certain edginess of being alone in the church had now started to niggle at her and she couldn't wait to leave. Peter Bristow was nowhere to be seen outside, making the silence of the still afternoon even more prominent. The only sounds to be heard were the faint rustle of the leaves on the trees and the distant barking of a dog some way down the road. As she reached the wooden gate at the end of the churchyard, Olive had a clear view of the vicarage on the other side of the lane, and she could also see the vicar, standing right there in full view with his hand raised ready to wave at her.

Olive flushed with anger, bloody cheek! The man obviously had no shame at all.

She turned on her heel as fast as she could and darted up the lane towards home, feeling both infuriated and scared. This was a man of God, the villagers were supposed to be able to trust him!

As she neared the cul-de-sac, Olive started to feel less afraid and more indignant about the events of the afternoon and by the time she stepped in to her kitchen, where Geoff was reading the newspaper, Olive was more than ready to give him her account of the whole incident.

Geoff listened intently, with grave concern spreading across his features. If there was one thing that really got him angry, it was men being disrespectful to women, and in his view Reverend Todd had seriously stepped over the line. He was going to sort him out.

"The dirty scoundrel", tutted Geoff, throwing aside his newspaper, "Whoever would have thought it of a man of the church?"

Olive hardly registered what her husband intended to do before he had grabbed his jacket and put on his heavy work boots. Geoff wasn't a violent man, and had no thoughts of driving his fists in to the middle-aged vicar, but instead would talk to him rationally with the hope that Reverend Todd would admit his vile deed and resign from his post in the parish. Hopefully then, poor Mrs. Hargreaves could move on.

It wasn't long before the girls showed up at the back door wanting to know where their father had gone without them. Olive tried to smile but something in her voice alerted her eldest daughter to the fact that something was wrong.

"Mother, what's the matter?' questioned Eileen, "Have you and father had a row?"

"Don't be silly dear", Olive offered, just a little too hastily, "He's got some business to attend to, and was in a hurry that's all. Now wash your hands and I'll get you both a glass of milk."

Barbara was first to the sink, sensing the prospect of a slice of fresh Victoria sponge, and failed to notice the strain in her mother's voice. Eileen was much sharper and peered in to her mother's eyes.

"Why do you look as though you're going to cry?" she asked quietly, out of her sister's earshot.

"Don't be silly, I've been peeling onions. I'm making us a chicken stew."

Eileen wasn't convinced, after all she saw no evidence that dinner preparations were underway and began to sense that something had happened while she'd been out riding her bicycle in the lane.

"But, how come..."

Olive cut her off in mid-sentence with a finger to the lips. She glanced at Barbara, who was drying her hands on a towel with her back to her mother and sister, and shook her head. The last thing she needed was her youngest daughter running around the houses telling everyone about their vicar's most inappropriate behaviour. Eileen nodded, a very intuitive girl she sensed that her mother would tell her the full story later, and nudged Barbara out of the way so that she could get to the sink. Minutes later the girls were sitting at the table with milk and cake, discussing whose turn it would be to tell the nightly ghost story that they had got into the habit of imparting. Their mother wandered in to the next room as her children bickered over Barbara's stories being too far-fetched and Eileen's being too scary.

Olive stood by the sitting room window, wringing a tea-towel in her hands for what seemed like a lifetime, but it was actually only an hour before Geoff came striding back up the lane, He looked worn out, as if he had suddenly aged by five years and had hit a premature mid-life crisis. Something had happened.

Ushering the girls outside under pretense of needing them to see if the hens had laid any eggs that afternoon, Olive instinctively started to make a pot of tea. She was quite taken aback when her husband announced that he would need something a bit stronger. In all their years of marriage, Olive had only known him drink alcohol at Christmas or on the rare occasion that they'd attended a family funeral.

As Geoff explained his confrontation with the clergyman, Olive's mouth involuntarily formed an "O".

It seemed that Mr. Hargreaves had also paid a visit to the vicarage and things had got quite heated, but certainly not in the way that Geoff had expected.

"It turns out that Mrs. Hargreaves and our vicar have been having an affair for a couple of years", said Geoff solemnly, "In fact she was ready to leave Stan and move in to the vicarage".

Olive gasped, "Oh poor Mrs. Todd, how on earth would she have coped with that devastating news, and how does that explain Mrs. Hargreaves' accusation this afternoon?"

"Oh you know," replied Geoff, "A woman scorned and all that. Seems that the Reverend was ready to break it all off and ask for a transfer to another church, so Mrs. Hargreaves wanted to make sure that it could never happen. She wanted him to lose his daughter and his reputation."

"So, I take it Mrs. Hargreaves has just confessed to her husband and that's why he went to see the vicar?" asked Olive, now beginning to feel she had a grasp on the situation.

"No, that's not it at all. You see that's the damnedest part of it," Geoff answered, now pulling out a second chair on which to support his legs while he removed his cumbersome boots, 'Apparently, Stan Hargreaves was having it away with Cynthia Todd and they were going to do a straight swap!. The only thing he's peeved about is the fact that the vicar's scuppered his plans!'

Olive took a huge intake of breath. It was all too much to comprehend. So many questions.

She shook her head. "What happens now then?"

'They reckon they'll all carry on with their lives as though nothing happened", grunted Geoff, still in a state of disbelief himself, "Tell you what love, it takes all sorts."

The secrets in this village just went from senseless to sordid, what on earth would they discover next?

Chapter Five
Honeysuckle Farm

If Olive, Geoff or any of their children looked down the cul-de-sac, right to the end, where it joined the winding lane, they could see Honeysuckle Farm.

It was quite an imposing layout, lots of barns and outbuildings set in acres of land, with the grand old farmhouse set at the front, near the roadside. At one time it had been an impressive example of Georgian architecture with pillars set each side of the entrance, long sash windows and chimneys at either end of the perfectly tiled red roof. Nowadays, if you looked closely, you could find signs of age and neglect. It was easy to spot paint peeling back from heavy wooden window sills, leaves and other debris spilling from the gutters and rust, which was now the most obvious component, on the decorative iron railings that ran along the tiny front garden.

Being a very handy man, Geoff had often wondered how the farmer, Bert Langtree, could bear to let his home fall in to such disrepair, but then he remembered how hard his own parents had worked to maintain their farm and he felt a pang of empathy. There was such a lot to do when you owned cattle and sheep. He recalled only having had a couple of holidays as a boy, and they were short, just a couple of days long when his uncle had come to help out on the small-holding. Of course, Geoff's parents had also employed farm hands who worked six days a week, so poor Bert Langtree must be exhausted with only one son to help out.

The farmer was a stout man, fairly tall and solidly built with strong forearms and a thick neck. He had thick greying curls that peeked out from under his flat cap and kept his trousers up with a piece of green twine. Bert's hands were rough and nobbled with callouses from continuous hard labour, but not once had Geoff or Olive seen him without a huge grin on his face. However, despite his cheerful disposition, Bert's forehead was furrowed with deep lines, giving rise for concern as to whether there may be some underlying issues which caused him to worry. His pride and joy, besides his farm, was a maroon two-door Morris Minor which sported soft cream leather seats and sparkling chrome trims. Every Sunday morning, just after dawn, Bert could be found polishing his prized possession until it gleamed like the silky outer skin of a red cherry.

From what Geoff had gathered in passing conversation, Honeysuckle Farm had been inherited from Bert's parents who had both now sadly passed away in the prime of their life. This information had not, however, been imparted by the farmer, but was actually offered by Stan Hargreaves their neighbour a couple of doors away. It hadn't been mentioned in spite or malicious gossiping, but more in passing conversation. Unfortunately, in light of recent events between the Hargreaves' and the Todds', little had been said between the two couples as both were just about as embarrassed as each other.

Mrs. Langtree was a strange creature in Geoff's opinion. He had often seen her travelling to town in a brown fur coat, a great striped thing with a huge collar, and vibrant purple lining which was just visible as she sashayed towards the bus. She didn't seem to realise that she looked like mutton dressed up as lamb, but instead walked with her head held high, a smug, almost superior look upon her face. Geoff wondered how Bert had come to marry such a woman, as the farmer was the friendliest chap he had met in the village so far, always ready to stop and chat, a joke or humorous proverb on his lips at every chance meeting. Perhaps he had married for money, Geoff pondered, there were plenty of men who would overlook a girl's personality if it aided their financial status. But the funny thing was, Geoff had never heard Bert Langtree say a single negative comment about his wife, and had only praised the way in which she ran the household, cooked to perfection and helped around the farm. Geoff supposed that if his friend was happy, she must be a different woman within her own family, as the image portrayed to the rest of the village was one of hostility and grandeur. It was almost as if Mrs. Langtree believed that one day some hot-shot Hollywood film producer would come along and whisk her away to a life of fame and fortune. For now, Geoff mused, she ought to realise that she was just a farmer's wife.

Despite their wives not being on the most familiar terms, Geoff and Bert gradually became very good chums and could often be spotted tinkering with the farm tractor, chatting over mugs of tea whilst sitting on a bale of hay outside the barn, or simply leaning on the huge wooden gate passing the time of day. There was a ten year age gap between the two men, Bert being the most senior, but it made not one iota of difference to their conversations, and it was almost as if they had grown up together. Of course, as men are inclined to do, they kept their discussions to everyday topics such as politics, motor-cars, sport and hobbies. Occasionally one would impart a piece of information about their home life to the other, but it would usually be in a general way, such as the details of a particularly good meal they had recently eaten, plans that they had for decorating their homes or a funny incident that had involved a family member. Gossip was most certainly not on Geoff and Bert's agenda.

Olive had tried to get Mrs. Langtree involved in the local community by offering to share a stall with her at the village fete one summer but, when the time had come to arrange their cakes and pies for sale, a note had been sent saying that Mrs. Langtree had a migraine and didn't feel up to it. It wasn't a total disappointment however, as her son Billy had arrived with baskets of fruit loaf and scones that his mother had baked the day before and carefully helped Olive to lay them out on the trestle table amongst the other stalls on the vicarage lawn. Olive still felt let down though, as she had to stand all day in the sunshine without assistance, whereas had she known earlier, she could have asked one of her sisters to come over for the day to help out. After several further failed attempts at trying to involve the farmer's wife in flower-arranging classes, a sponsored walk, afternoon tea in town and a bus trip to the seaside, Olive gave up. It just seemed that Mrs. Langtree thought herself too upper-class to become involved with the day to day lives of the villagers.

The Langtree's were regular attendees at church and those occasions were the one time of the week when the farmer's wife seemed happy to converse with the rest of the villagers. Always dressed in her brown fur coat, come rain or shine, the farmer's wife would smile politely, feigning interest in the conversations around her and all the time still managing to stay a little aloof from the rest of the group. Other times, at the village shop, waiting at the bus-stop or at a social event, she was decidedly colder towards those around her and would keep the chitchat to a minimum. From Geoff, Olive had learned that Mrs. Langtree's first name was Agatha, but they were on far from close terms and her Christian name was never used as it seemed as though there was an invisible line between the two women and it was one that Olive had little wish to cross. She did sometimes think it would be fun to have the Langtree's as close friends, another couple to go out for a meal with or invite round for a drink when they had occasion to celebrate, but the slightly frosty stare with which the farmer's wife regarded other women did little to ease the tension between them.

It was difficult to put an age to Agatha Langtree, perhaps somewhere in her late forties Olive guessed, as the farmer's wife always had very heavily applied face powder and dressed up in fashions intended for a much younger woman. The dark sunglasses that she wore on every summer's day only added to her eccentricity, as did the pointed court shoes, over-sized handbags and paste gemstones on her fingers. Olive did, now and again, try to conjure up a topic in which to engage Agatha in small talk but it always felt rather one-sided with mono-symbolic responses and rolling of the eyes.

Mrs. Langtree did have one good friend who could regularly be seen pulling up outside the farm gate on her bicycle but nobody seemed to know who she was or where she lived. A very plain young woman, make-up free with a boyish figure, the lady would visit for exactly an hour and then peddle off out of the village in the same direction as that from which she had arrived. But, apart from that one visitor, Agatha Langtree seemed to live a lonely existence, shut up in the rambling farmhouse with nobody for company until her husband and young son came in for their meals, with only shopping trips in to town to detract from the day to day life of a busy working farm.

Occasionally Bert would venture up the cul-de-sac to ask his friend's advice on fixing some piece of equipment or to take a peek at the latest creation that Geoff happened to be building in his shed, but more often than not it would be Geoff who strolled down to the farm for a chat. Geoff also liked to see what the latest agricultural developments were, as farming was in his blood and he missed the days of his youth where he had sometimes spent a whole afternoon tackling sheep in order to shear their fleeces, or following his father's precise instructions on how to brand the newest additions to their growing herd of cattle. Bert Langtree's farm was on a much smaller scale to that of Geoff's family, but Geoff was still impressed at his friend's depth of knowledge and passion for his line of work.

The only difference between the two men was the fact that Bert Langtree liked a drink. Now Geoff wasn't completely tea-total and had been known to imbibe a little too much real ale at Christmas but Bert's drinking was more of a ritual and every evening he looked forward to putting his feet up in front of the log fire with a bottle of whisky at his side. Over the years Bert's drinking had taken its toll on him and now, in his middle-aged years, the tell-tale signs were beginning to appear, giving his cheeks a permanent rosy glow and feathery red veins now creeping slowly along the sides of his nose. Geoff thought it sad that the farmer needed to take comfort in alcohol but reasoned that Bert worked a darn sight harder than a lot of men his age and therefore deserved to indulge in whatever took his fancy.

Bert Langtree seldom talked about his past, seeming more inclined to look towards a hopeful future but, when he did, he told Geoff tales of the days when he would ride his Tiger Cub motorbike to the next village where he would slow down at the gate of a large grey house. That was where his wife to be had lived, Bert said, the love of his life, his Maude. On the first instance that his friend had mentioned a romance with Maude, Geoff had been rather taken aback that the woman to whom he was devoted was not actually the one that he had married. However, being a good listener, he allowed the tale to continue unravelling over a period of a few weeks, never casting judgement nor pressing for more details. Then one day, after a couple of hours helping Geoff to paint some wooden money boxes he'd made for the children, Bert felt comfortable enough in his friend's company to expand on the story of his marriage.

"She was the most beautiful girl in the whole county was Maude", smiled Bert, "A real gem."

Geoff nodded politely, waiting for the farmer to continue, he was a patient man by nature.

"We started courting when she was eighteen. It was just a peck on the cheek in the evenings, you know how it is, and then one day she just didn't turn up. We were supposed to be going for a ride on my bike that evening, nowhere special, just a ride in the country, but I was really looking forward to it."

Geoff put down the paint pot that he'd been holding and turned to face Bert.

"What happened?" he coaxed.

"Well, I kept riding past, night after night, and then finally plucked up the courage to go and knock on the door. Her father wasn't surprised to see me, nice chap too, it seemed he'd known about me all along."

"Did he stop you from seeing Maude?" asked Geoff cautiously, knowing how old-fashioned and protective some fathers could be about their daughters, himself included.

"Oh no, he was fine about that. Very sad it was, Maude had contracted TB and become ill very quickly you see. She was hospitalised but didn't see the month out. She passed away on October 2nd, which just happens to be my birthday too."

Geoff cast his eyes downwards, not quite knowing what to say. Luckily Bert continued.

"Anyway, over the months I ended up getting friendly with her father, he was in to his bikes as well so we had a lot to talk about. There was no mother, just another daughter, Agatha. And that's the girl I ended up marrying, not as pretty as her sister but a good 'un all the same. Suffers with terrible moods does my Agatha, she's always been highly strung but, with her poor old Dad advancing in years and no other bugger interested in courting her, I made him a promise that I'd take care of her. We don't always see eye to eye, and she's still jealous of her sister's memory, but we muddle along alright."

Geoff nodded, now it all made sense, the sadness in Bert's eyes and the mismatched marriage.

The Langtree's actually had two sons, as Geoff was soon to discover, but only the youngest one, Billy, was at home. He was the apple of his father's eye and was a real credit to his parents. Hard-working, fun and handsome, Billy Langtree idolised his father and had inherited both Bert's natural talent with animals and his passion for Honeysuckle Farm. At eighteen years old, Billy was becoming somewhat of a local attraction amongst the girls of the village, and rumours of his muscly torso and rugged good looks had spread to the neighbouring hamlets, bringing adolescent young ladies flocking to the farm under pretense of needing butter, milk or eggs, just so that they might catch the young farmer's eye. Billy, however, had no interest in the girls who tracked him down, he was saving himself for someone special, someone like Geoff and Olive's daughter Eileen who, although several years his junior, was pretty, smart and also shared his love of animals. Billy knew that it would be a long wait before Eileen felt the hormonal stirrings that turned a girl into a young lady, but he was willing to wait. In his eyes Eileen was perfect and perfect was worth holding out for.

Bert had explained that his elder son, Ben, was away 'serving' which made him immensely proud, although it was more often that Geoff enquired after Ben's well-being rather than his father broaching the subject. Geoff reasoned that the Langtree's must miss their boy terribly, it was obviously a painful topic of conversation for them. Bert had said that Ben was in Surrey, and twice a year he and his wife would make the journey down there to visit, just for a day, staying overnight and driving back the next morning. Geoff thought that Ben must be in a very important regiment of the army if he never came home on leave, and wondered if the bright lights of London were more of an attraction to him at weekends then spending time in this quiet village, with nothing but one public house within a three mile radius. Still, it was a shame, Bert had obviously hoped that his two son's would work the farm together when he finally decided to retire.

The first time the Langtree's made the long trip to Surrey since becoming acquainted with Geoff and his family, was at the beginning of a long, hard winter. Frost was just starting to harden the ground and extra hay had to be strewn across the floor of the cattle stalls for added warmth, a task which both Eileen and Barbara had helped with eagerly after school. Eileen especially was happy to spend time at the farm, as she had been allowed to take her pick of the kittens born a few weeks earlier, and carefully watched their progress as she decided between a scruffy tabby female and a cheeky black and white male.

During his parent's absence, Billy was going to manage things alone for the couple of days while they were away but Geoff had promised to help out after work, while Olive had insisted that the young man join her family for meals. As Bert and his wife loaded up their Morris Minor car on the Saturday morning, Geoff strolled across the lane to wish them a safe journey. He could clearly see Bert's wife dressed up in her brown fur coat again, dolled up to the nines with her hair piled into a neat bun and bright red lipstick smeared across her thin lips. Geoff, shook his head, even from a man's perspective he could see it was all show and no real glamour, for the fur coat had a gaping hole at the shoulder seam, the red lipstick had smudged becoming stuck on Mrs. Langtree's teeth and the hem of her skirt hung down far too low, showing where the satin lining had clearly come undone. Still, he thought, none of my business.

"Take care on the road, and don't worry about Billy, I'm off work tomorrow and can lend a hand around here", he assured Bert, "you just go off and enjoy spending time with Ben'.

'Thanks Geoff", replied the farmer, grasping his friend's hand and shaking it firmly, 'That's a weight off my mind, although our Billy's a good lad and I know he'll be fine."

Geoff nodded, "He's a credit to you Bert, as I'm sure is Ben."

A momentary shadow seemed to be cast upon the farmer's face and he flinched, suddenly stuck for words and unable to respond. Geoff leaned forward and put a hand on Bert's shoulder.

"I know you must be eager to get going", he said kindly, "Enjoy yourselves."

Again Bert looked lost for words and simply nodded before climbing in to the driver's seat.

Later that day, Billy arrived at Olive and Geoff's clutching a bunch of wild poppies he'd picked from the hedgerow on his way back from bringing the cattle in for milking.

"I thought these might look pretty on your dresser", he said shyly, handing the flowers to Olive.

'Why, how thoughtful", she gushed, "Now sit yourself down and help yourself to a cup of tea. Dinner will be ready in just a few minutes, it's beef stew and dumplings."

"Smells delicious", replied Billy genuinely, "It's very kind of you to invite me."

"Nonsense", chuckled Geoff, now pulling out a chair and seating himself at the young man's side, 'We're very glad to have you here son. Now let's see how much of our Olive's stew you can manage, eh?'

The two girls suddenly appeared at the kitchen door, Eileen shy and demure, Barbara loud and brash, and seated themselves around the long wooden table. The meal was served and general conversation began.

"How long has your brother been in Surrey?" asked Olive, genuinely wondering how Billy's poor mother had coped with her eldest son leaving the nest.

"A couple of years", replied Billy, "He'll be there for another eight I think."

"Must be quite a career he's getting himself there", quipped Geoff, 'Marvellous."

Billy looked puzzled and then laughed nervously, 'I suppose you could call it that", he replied.

Olive gave Geoff a sharp kick under the table and shot him a hard look, Billy obviously didn't want to talk about his brother's vocation in the army. Perhaps there was an element of jealousy in that Ben had a life of opportunity ahead of him while Billy was stuck on the farm, Olive wondered. She of all people knew how two siblings could be complete opposites, you only had to take Eileen and Barbara as an example. Maybe it was the same with Ben and Billy Langtree.

Meanwhile Geoff was pondering the exact same scenario. He could picture Ben in his smart uniform with boots polished to perfection, maybe even becoming officer material if he kept a level head.

Luckily, just as Geoff was deciding whether to probe further in to Ben Langtree's military career, baby Godfrey started to cry and everyone's attention was drawn to the sobbing child.

"Here, let me take him", offered Billy, reaching over to pull the tiny boy out of his wooden high-chair.

Godfrey immediately shut off the waterworks and gazed up in to Billy's smiling face.

"You've got a real knack there", smiled Olive, "He doesn't take to everyone."

Billy gently jiggled the baby up and down on his lap, "He's a smashing lad, Olive, I can't wait to have a family of my own." As soon as the words had been spoken Billy blushed. 'I mean, erm, when I find the right girl of course and not yet, I'm too young…"

On the other side of the table Barbara giggled, she was at the age where any mention of girlfriends or boyfriends was funny. Olive gave her a warning look and she settled back down in her seat, but with a hand over her mouth to stem the laughter that wanted to escape from her throat.

Billy passed a happy Godfrey over to Olive and finished his meal, still with a red tinge to his cheeks.

"I'd best be off", he said, 'Lots to do tomorrow. Thank you for the smashing dinner.'

"You're very welcome lad", gushed Olive, "Geoff will you see Billy out, I need to bath Godfrey."

The two men stepped outside and took in the starry sky above them. The moon was full and cast long a yellow glow across the lane. Honeysuckle Farm was clearly visible, every window in darkness.

Geoff patted Billy on the shoulder, "I'll see you bright and early in the morning son."

Billy nodded, "Thanks again for your hospitality Geoff, I'll see you tomorrow"

Geoff watched as the younger man made his way home, carefully latched the farm gate behind him, and then made a fuss of the two barking collies as they raced to greet him. A light went on at the rear of the farmhouse and only then did Geoff go back inside and turn the key in his own door.

Early the next day, Geoff set off down to the farm with a parcel of ham and pickle sandwiches and two slices of Olive's fruit cake to share with Billy when they took a break from their morning's labour.

As he reached the farm gate, Geoff could see Billy already hard at work, the sleeves of his checked shirt rolled up to the elbow and hard-wearing rubber boots pulled up over his work trousers. The cows had been milked and he was now busily collecting eggs in the chicken coop at the side of the house.

"What do you need me to do?" shouted Geoff as he approached the younger man.

"Well, you're a far better carpenter than either me or my Dad", returned Billy, "Would you mind taking a look at the fence near the brook? That bull's been trying to get out again and I'm afraid that if we leave it any longer, he'll be off chasing Mr. Adams' herd."

Geoff nodded, "Happy to oblige, I'll just fetch the tools and get on to it right away."

And so, with Geoff busy at the far end of the Langtree's boundary field and Billy occupied with feeding the sheep, cattle and chickens, they had little chance for conversation until mid-day. It had taken Geoff a good couple of hours to repair the bull's damage and after that he had set to work strengthening the heavy wooden slats on the farm gate, where he had noticed the gaps were becoming wide enough to allow the farm dogs to jump through. It was with a hearty appetite that he now joined Billy in the farmhouse kitchen for a mug of tea and shared lunch. This was the first occasion on which Geoff had spent any length of time in the Langtree's house, as usually he would find Bert already outside hard at work. He took in the surroundings with a mix of intrigue and bewilderment. The kitchen into which he had been ushered was huge, easily the size of the whole downstairs in his own cottage, but the furnishings were more practical than decorative. A long wooden bench ran along the wall nearest the door, serving as a convenient place for the men of the house to take off their boots and store them neatly underneath. There were worn wooden units along the window wall, a huge dresser filled with crockery on the opposite side and in the centre of the room stood an enormous oak table with enough chairs to seat a family of ten. From the ceiling hung a long wooden clothes airer, which was full of shirts, undergarments and overalls.

Geoff took off his muddy boots and made his way over to the sink to wash his hands. As he soaped his arms, he glanced out of the wide panoramic window and caught Billy's reflection behind him.

"So, what's on the agenda for this afternoon?" Geoff asked, hoping that it would be something a little less strenuous. He was by no means a lazy man, but the last thing he needed was to go in to work on Monday morning with a stiff back and aching arms.

"Oh, I thought we could chop up that fallen tree into logs", chirped Billy, trying not to laugh.

The look on Geoff's face must have given away his inner thoughts, as soon Billy was chuckling out loud and shaking his head, "Just joking, I'll be fine if you want to go home and put your feet up", he said.

Geoff dried his hands and gave the lad a friendly punch on the arm 'You had me going there", he chortled, 'But I'll gladly stay and help you clean out the milking stalls, it'll keep me out from under Olive's feet."

Billy nodded, 'Thanks, that'd be great. I'll have time to fix a meal for Mum and Dad when they get home then. They'll be tired after the long drive back."

"You're a credit to them", said Geoff thoughtfully, "You, and your brother Ben. Great boys."

Billy suddenly gave Geoff a strange look, which he didn't know how to interpret.

'Sorry lad, did I say something out of turn?" asked Geoff kindly, 'I meant no offence."

'It's nothing", replied Billy slowly, letting out a huge breath, 'nothing important."

'Now you know, if there's something wrong you can tell me,' offered the older man 'You know what they say, a problem shared and all that."

Billy shrugged, "It's nothing really", he murmured, "Just a long time since I've seen our Ben."

Geoff coughed and tactfully moved over to the table to unwrap the packet of sandwiches. He wasn't sure what to say, and waited for the young man to carry on. Nothing came.

"How many sugars?" asked Billy, turning his attention to the teapot.

"No sugar, and just a spot of milk if you don't mind", Geoff answered, sitting down at the table.

No more was said about the older Langtree boy that lunchtime. Instead the two men talked about the weather, motorbikes and the price that farmers were currently getting for milk sales. They ate a hearty meal and it wasn't long before the topic once again turned back to Billy's brother.

"That's Ben", said Billy pointing at a faded photograph perched on the dresser amongst the plates.

Geoff stood up to get a better look, and was surprised to note that Ben looked no more than a couple of years older than his brother. With thick dark curls he was the spitting image of his mother, whereas Ben looked much more like their father. It was a typical family shot, with all four family members huddled together smiling for the camera.

"He's a good looking fellow isn't he?" noted Geoff, "Tall too."

Billy stood up and took the picture out of the older man's grasp, "He's a rum 'un", he said, setting the photo back on the dresser shelf, "Always had to have his own way."

With that, he collected up their empty mugs and dropped them in to the sink, before pulling on his muddy boots and trudging across the farmyard to the milking shed.

Geoff followed silently, wondering what had provoked such a sudden mood change, there was obviously an issue between Billy and his older brother. As he caught up with Billy, Geoff tried to smooth things over by changing the subject to something less personal. He gave the lad a poke in the ribs and chuckled.

'What's the best way to get the smell of cow dung off your clothes then?" he laughed.

"Burn them", retorted Billy, recovering some of his poise, "Or buy new ones!"

They worked companionably side by side for the remainder of the afternoon, Billy shoveling straw and muck from the floor of the milking stalls and Geoff scrubbing it before putting a fresh layer down. The cows were still out in the field, where they would stay until late afternoon, which made the men's work less cumbersome. When the time came for Billy to fetch them back for milking, he whistled to the two collie dogs who were lounging in the barn doorway, and asked Geoff if he had time to walk up the lane with him to herd the cattle home. Geoff eagerly agreed and they set off on the ten minute walk to the field.

"I've never understood how a cow will stand in a field all day and then suddenly decide it needs a crap as soon as its feet hit the road", laughed Geoff, "One of the world's great mysteries."

Billy chuckled, "You're so right about that. Although, I'd never really thought of it before."

The men arrived at the field and, being experienced in handling the cows, soon had the herd plodding back down the lane to empty their udders. Sure enough, within two minutes of hitting the road, three of the cows in the lead pack lifted their tails and relieved themselves. Billy turned to Geoff who was already starting to grin in an 'I told you so' kind of way, and both men found themselves laughing all the way back to the farm. They settled the cows in their stalls and began the milking process.

"I haven't half enjoyed working with you today son", shouted Geoff over the top of the rump of a cow.

"Don't let my Dad hear you say that", joked Billy, "He'll have you down here every spare minute."

"Must be hard just the two of you."

Billy turned slowly around to face Geoff and the older man could see clearly that his face was flushed, but whether in anger or embarrassment Geoff couldn't rightly tell.

"My brother is serving time", Billy finally offered.

'Yes lad, in the army. But what's the issue?" Geoff cautiously asked, trying not to sound judgmental.

Billy shook his head, 'No, not in the army Geoff, in prison. He's inside for armed robbery."

Geoff took a step back, hardly believing what was being said, "But, I thought…."

"Mum and Dad never actually said the army", explained Billy, "People have always just presumed. Our Ben is inside for robbing a post office and wounding the clerk. He got ten years."

"But why?" cried Geoff, now becoming quite alarmed "Why did he need to do that?"

"His gambling addiction", answered Billy, now sinking down on to the cold brick floor of a milking stall,

"Our Ben had run up hundreds of pounds of debt, horse-racing, poker, cock fights, you name it and he put money on it. Then one day these blokes turned up demanding money, all heavy like. Well, our Dad, being a bit naïve told them he'd pay them off over a couple of months, you know, thinking it was a few pounds that Ben was owing. When he found out exactly how much had to be paid back to those loan sharks, Dad nearly had heart failure. That's when Ben took matters in to his own hands, took my Dad's shotgun and decided to rob the post office in Nareborough. He thought it was far enough away not to be recognised. His plan was to do one job a month until all the money was paid off and nobody would be the wiser. Seems he hadn't thought it through and things went wrong."

"And what about the loan sharks?" asked Geoff quietly, "Who will pay them off?"

"Oh, that's all sorted", sniffed Billy, now standing up and brushing off his trousers, "Mum sold all her jewellery and paid off every last penny."

Geoff slowly put an arm around Billy's shoulder, his mind racing at what he'd just been told.

Maybe Olive was right, he thought, perhaps this village IS full of secrets.

Chapter Six
Rita Butterworth

By the following Winter, little Godfrey had taken his first steps and Olive found that she now had to juggle her daily chores while keeping a watchful eye on her son. Of course, as parents, Olive and Geoff were delighted that Godfrey was learning new skills every week but it also meant that they now had to remember to lift their belongings out of reach of his curious fingers and make sure that cupboards and doors were securely closed. There had already been a couple of occasions where Godfrey had managed to open the kitchen drawers, flinging wooden spoons and other utensils noisily across the floor. There had also been a few curious incidents where she had turned around from the sink to find her young boy covered in flour or grasping a block of thick yellow butter in his tiny hands, which had puzzled Olive no end as she knew that those items had been safely out of reach on the work surface or kitchen table. She initially suspected that Barbara was involved but, upon interrogation, the red-headed girl vehemently denied being anywhere near the kitchen or her brother. Still, Olive was not convinced and decided to keep a tight rein on her youngest daughter.

During the summer months, Olive and Geoff's daughters had spent many hours playing outdoors after school but, now that the evenings were colder and darker, they were spending much more of their time in the house and subsequently Barbara was easily bored. Eileen was never a problem, as she studiously completed her homework, helped her mother in the kitchen and played with her baby brother. It was seldom that Olive ever had to ask Eileen for help, as she always seemed to be there, knowing exactly what needed to be done with never a negative word. Olive had long ago thought that Barbara should have been a boy. Although cute with her curly golden locks, blue eyes and freckled cheeks, Barbara insisted on wearing only trousers when not in school and would wrestle with anger every time her mother insisted on her putting on a smart dress for Sunday school. And instead of playing at tea parties or pushing a doll in in its pram like the other village girls of the same age, Barbara could usually be found climbing trees, watching the older boys tinkering with their motorbikes or playing practical jokes on the more elderly members of the community. In Barbara's book, the more you told her not to do something, or gave her a harsh scolding, the more determined she would be to seek revenge.

It was during those long winter months, just when Olive was at the end of her tether, that Barbara became ill. At first it was just a cough, frequent but not severe, but as the days passed Olive and Geoff could see no improvement in their youngest daughter, with her eventually having difficulty breathing and being unable to sleep due to the tightness in her chest. The local doctor suggested taking Barbara to see a specialist, which was arranged with no real sense of urgency but did not take long.

A diagnosis revealed that Barbara was suffering from bronchitis and would need to stay off school for several months. Olive was given medication to administer daily, and a list of gentle breathing exercises accompanied the hospital notes given by the consultant. Both Olive and Geoff began to feel a slight sense of guilt that they had blamed Barbara for much of the mischief in their household but also secretly worried that with Barbara at home every day, there would be even more disruption to their daily lives.

'Do you reckon you could home school her until she's better?' asked Geoff tentatively one evening.

Olive shot him a look that definitely said 'No', but when she opened her mouth to speak her words were much less harsh, "It would be difficult with Godfrey and all the household tasks..." she started.

"Just an idea", responded Geoff sympathetically, "I can come home earlier and give her some lessons in the evenings, just need to get this large order out of the factory first."

Olive shook her head, "No, that's too much for you", she said, rubbing her husband's back, "Maybe I can ask Dolly to come and stay, we could fix up another bed in the girl's room..."

Geoff wasn't convinced, "Your Dolly wasn't much of a scholar really was she?" he started, but then thought better of pursuing the matter further and returned to his evening newspaper.

Olive just rolled her eyes and put the kettle on. For now the issue was closed.

As they pondered the dilemma of Barbara's education, a visit from Mrs. Hamilton, who lived a few doors away, shed new hope upon the situation. According to their neighbour, there was a lady living half way between the cul-de-sac and the church who used to be the schoolmistress of a prestigious girl's school in town. She had often given extra lessons to the children in the village for a very reasonable fee and, Mrs. Hamilton assured them, she was a very strict teacher who also might be able to discipline Barbara in ways that had not yet been attainable. Olive and Geoff felt a deep sense of curiosity. Surely this could be the very type of education that Barbara needed, a teacher whose attention would be solely focused on her with the additional benefit of being able to rest at home in the afternoons. Mrs. Hamilton kindly offered to visit the schoolmistress on Olive and Geoff's behalf, with a view to securing a meeting the very next day.

Within the hour, Mrs. Hamilton returned with positive news. The schoolmistress would gladly come up to meet Barbara's parents and very much looked forward to meeting them. She would come over the next evening when Geoff returned home from work as, she had pointed out, it was very important to meet both parents before any kind of agreement on Barbara's education could be settled upon.

Just before the appointed time, Olive carefully laid out her best china teacups, brewed a fresh pot of tea and arranged slices of fruit cake on a pretty glass platter.

"Bloody hell Mother", grumbled Geoff, "Anyone would think the Queen was coming to tea, it's only some doddery old school ma'm you know. No need to go to all this palaver."

"I just want her to have a good impression of us", muttered Olive as she fussed with the tablecloth and napkins, "Barbara's lessons are very important Geoff, you should know that better than anyone."

"Mmm, but she might charge extra if she thinks we can afford it", replied her husband.

"Don't be silly........." started Olive, but she was unable to finish her sentence as there was suddenly a sharp tap at the door, interrupting her chain of thought.

As his wife turned on her heel to answer the door, Geoff swiftly removed the napkins from the coffee table and returned them to the sideboard drawer. "Women", he mused, "As long as I live I'll never understand them." As voices approached, Geoff quickly spun around to catch a glimpse of himself in the mirror over the fireplace. Not only did he see his own reflection, but spied the wide eyes of Barbara peeping around the door behind him. She flushed as her eyes met those of her father and scampered away before he had time to give her the signal to disappear up to bed.

"This is Miss. Rita Butterworth", said Olive as she entered the room, followed by a very small bird-like woman dressed from head to toe in grey. Her hair was light brown tinged with occasional white streaks, and she wore a pale pink lipstick which had obviously been very hastily applied as it failed to stay within the boundaries of her lips. She smelled of moth-balls and pee.

"Very pleased to meet you", said Geoff, now holding out his hand, "I'll just get some napkins."

"How do you do?" replied the little woman, showing crooked yellowed teeth as she smiled "Lovely home you have here, very cozy." Her voice was high-pitched and upper-class.

Rita Butterworth had a very fuss-free and rational approach when it came to education. She would teach Barbara all of the subjects that she would be expected to learn at school, for a total of three hours every day. Each lesson would be divided into forty-five minute slots with fifteen minutes at the end of each one purely devoted to discussion and review. She expected a reasonable fee, paid weekly in advance. In return she would provide books and lesson plans which would need to be returned to her once Barbara was well enough to resume her regular classes at school. In addition, Ms. Butterworth made it perfectly clear that she would not tolerate fools and expected Barbara to be both diligent and respectful when it came to her new tutor. Olive and Geoff glanced at each other, they'd have to have words with their daughter.

And so, it was arranged that Rita Butterworth would arrive at 9am every weekday morning and deliver lessons to Barbara until noon. Thereafter, the young girl would rest during the afternoon and have the weekends free to play with her elder sister. Barbara didn't seem to be alarmed at the news that she would still have to study despite being at home due to illness, but she wasn't over-enthusiastic at finding out that her new teacher was so advanced in years.

The arrangement worked well for a couple of days. Olive busied herself in the kitchen or took little Godfrey out for a stroll to the village shop, while Rita Butterworth tried her best to impart some knowledge to Barbara, albeit under duress from the young girl. On the fourth day, however, baby Godfrey decided to start teething and no matter how his mother tried to pacify him, he just would not stop howling. Unused to such disturbances, Ms. Butterworth rose from her seat in the sitting room and peered around the kitchen door to see what all the commotion was about. Barbara, being a devilish child, took full advantage of her distracted teacher at that point and began to sketch stick people on to her mother's white linen tablecloth with her fountain pen. Needless to say, both mother and tutor were furious when the terrible deed was discovered and lessons, for that day, were drawn to a close.

Later that evening, as Geoff finished his dinner, Olive recounted Barbara's behaviour earlier in the day and asked her husband what he thought was the solution. Geoff was quiet for a few minutes, pulling at his braces and scratching his head, then he leaned back in his chair and gave a great sigh.

"Why not send her to Ms. Butterworth's house for instruction, there'd be far less distractions and you wouldn't need to worry about replacing the tablecloth every second day", he offered.

Olive smiled, Geoff had a good idea, as long as Barbara behaved herself at the schoolteacher's house.

The next morning, as Ms. Butterworth laid out Barbara's exercise books on the coffee table, Olive sidled into the sitting room and began to impart her husband's grand idea.

"I'm sure that Barbara would become a much better student without all the distractions at home", she enthused, "Your house must be much quieter than here, and I'll be sure to pick her up on time."

The tutor eyed Olive warily, taking her time before responding.

"I suppose you do have a valid point", she finally replied, remembering the dreadful headache she had nursed only the previous day when Olive's baby had screamed for most of the morning. "As long as she promises not to touch ANYTHING, and takes her lessons seriously."

"Of course", Olive nodded, hoping that Barbara wouldn't embarrass her, "The slightest sign of trouble and she'll have her father to answer to. That's settled then."

Therefore, the following day, instead of clearing the coffee table and making a pot of tea for Ms. Butterworth, Olive wrapped herself, Barbara and Godfrey in warm clothing and set off for the walk to the schoolmistress's house on the other side of the village. It was a particularly frosty morning and Barbara did nothing but complain. So, by the time Olive reached her destination, all she wanted to do was drop off her young child at the teacher's door and scuttle back to the warmth of her own snug house. It was just as well, as there was certainly no warm welcome to step inside for a moment, in fact, Ms. Butterworth barely opened the door wide enough to allow Barbara to pass through. Olive shrugged and set off back through the sleepy village. Barbara would be fine, at least she would now be able to concentrate fully on her lessons. Olive just hoped there was no mischief afoot.

At noon, after a morning of sweeping, dusting and changing the bed sheets, Olive once again found herself at the schoolteacher's house, ready to collect her daughter. As before, Rita Butterworth opened the door just a fraction and closed it again once Barbara was at her mother's side. Unused to such behaviour, Olive wondered what was behind the door, maybe Ms. Butterworth had a large dog, she asked her child.

"No", replied Barbara, "She doesn't have any pets."

As the walk was a cold and windy one, Olive refrained from quizzing Barbara further and instead concentrated on getting her children indoors to the warmth of their kitchen. Both Barbara and Godfrey will be hungry after all this fresh air, thought Olive, I'll toast us some teacakes with lashings of butter. It wasn't until mid-afternoon, when the plates were cleared away and both children had taken a nap, that Olive had the chance to question Barbara about Ms. Butterworth's rather abrupt exchange.

"She was really nice to me", smiled Barbara, pulling some books out of her little cotton bag, "We talked about all sorts of things and look Mother, she even gave me this."

Olive stretched out her hand to take a rather battered looking book from her daughter. It appeared to be very old and smelled as though something had died between the pages.

"Oh dear", frowned Olive, fanning herself with her free hand, "I don't think you should have that!"

"But Ms. Butterworth said it was a story book from Victorian times and I want to keep it", yelled Barbara, stamping her foot upon the floor and shaking her ringlets franticly, "You spoil everything!"

"But it might make you poorly dear", said Olive trying to calm her child, "The pages have mould on them, which is really not good for your chest." But before she could pry the offending article away from her daughter, Barbara had snatched back the book and was hurtling upstairs with it at a fast pace.

Olive started to follow and then remembered the hospital consultant's advice. He had suggested that conflict be avoided to minimise Barbara's coughing. The more she became agitated, the worse the spasms would be, so the family must ensure a happy environment with little for the girl to become upset about.

With Godfrey now starting to niggle in his cot, Olive turned away from the direction of the girl's room and headed instead to heat up some milk for her son. She would leave Barbara alone to overcome her tantrum, and Geoff could help her to see reason when he returned later, besides Eileen would be back from school soon and Olive knew that Barbara would become distracted with news of what her sister would be playing in the upcoming nativity play and then she might forget those old and tattered books.

As it was, Geoff had news of his own that night, which meant that he and Olive sat talking by the fire for much longer than usual after dinner. It was nothing life-changing, just word of one of the foundry bosses getting married, and moving to Australia, but it was enough for Olive to become distracted and she neglected to tell Geoff about their youngest daughter's temper tantrum that afternoon.

Next morning, as Olive pulled back the curtains in Eileen and Barbara's bedroom, she noticed the horrid book lying on the floor between the two beds. She silently stooped down and picked it up between thumb and forefinger, trying carefully not to touch the mottled edges, and took it outside to the dustbin. It wasn't long before an irate freckled face appeared at the kitchen door.

"Where's my book? demanded Barbara, 'I want it back. Mother you had no right to take it."

Olive sighed, here we go again, she thought, trying to appease her daughter with the promise of pancakes with golden syrup for afternoon tea.

As they headed out into the blustery wind to Ms. Butterworth's house, Olive tried to explain about bacteria and how the pages of that dirty Victorian book might make Barbara ill should she keep it.

"It doesn't matter anyway", snapped the young girl defiantly, "There are thousands of books in my teacher's house, and she said I can borrow any that I want, whenever I want. She has so many that yesterday I sat upon a mountain made of books and nearly fell off, so there!"

Olive stopped walking and took a moment to look at her daughter's face. It was usually so easy to tell when Barbara was exaggerating or telling a lie but today her face was defiant and there was nothing in her expression that suggested she was making up a tall tale.

"Where exactly was this mountain of books?" enquired Olive, "In Miss. Butterworth's house?"

Barbara suddenly looked rather sheepish. "Oh, er, I promised not to tell."

Olive picked up her pace, pushing Godfrey's pram faster and faster while Barbara struggled to keep up at her side. Not far now, and she would be able to question Rita Butterworth about the child's claims.

On opening her front door, the schoolmistress must have sensed that something was playing on Olive's mind. Instead of giving her usual courteous nod as she welcomed her pupil inside, Rita Butterworth pulled the door closed behind her and stood on the doorstep with one eyebrow raised.

"Morning, Ms. Butterworth", began Olive, "I wondered if I could talk to you about something that Barbara said, it involves some books."

"Oh, children can make up such stories, can't they?" replied the teacher, "What on earth has she been telling you?"

Olive thought it strange that the old lady had become defensive before she had even explained her reason for concern, but she was assured by the older woman that there was no need to be alarmed. She simply had a large collection of literature, that was all, Ms. Butterworth clarified.

"As for climbing up them, dearie me, how ridiculous", she added as she ushered Barbara inside.

Olive seemed satisfied that this was another one of her daughter's pretensions and turned to leave.

Over the next few weeks, Barbara seemed to settle in to her studies quite well and Olive found that her daughter's behaviour at home had become less stressful than usual. Most afternoons with their lunch over and Godfrey taking a nap, the young girl would play quietly with her toys or lie on her bed with a story book. There were fewer tantrums and much more interest in learning. One evening Geoff raised his observations to his wife.

"Seems Ms. Butterworth has curbed our Barbara's attitude", he remarked to Olive.

"Yes, I can certainly see a big difference", replied his wife, "She seems to be enjoying her studies too."

"Mmm" muttered Geoff, "Can't help thinking there might be a storm brewing though love, she hasn't been this well behaved since we confiscated her bike for that week in the summer."

"Don't tempt fate", chuckled Olive, "Perhaps she's starting to realise that her education's important."

"Maybe", let's see how long she can go without getting up to something."

They both laughed, neither believing that life could continue so harmoniously for long.

Later that week, as Olive and Eileen rushed around getting ready for church service and Sunday school, Barbara came stomping downstairs with a scowl on her face. She was wearing thick wool trousers but her feet were bare.

"Why can't I come?" She moaned. "I feel better now and I want to hear the stories about baby Jesus."

"You're not well enough yet", chided her mother, turning the child around and leading her back upstairs, "You have to stay here with your Dad and Godfrey. Now let's go and find you some warm socks."

Barbara huffed and shook her ginger ringlets furiously as she headed towards her bedroom. Olive tutted to herself and opened the huge chest of drawers, searching for something to cover her child's feet.

"Here we are", she exclaimed, "Lovely red pair, these will keep your toes snuggly."

Barbara relented a little and sat on the bed while her mother helped to put on the socks. However, just as Olive was sliding her daughter's trouser leg up above the ankle in order to pull up a sock, she noticed a huge purple bruise covering a couple of inches of skin.

"What on earth have you done?" she questioned, "Did you fall over, love?"

"It happened at Ms. Butterworth's house on Friday", mumbled Barbara, "It was my own fault, I was trying to put something back on the shelf and I slipped."

Olive frowned, "Was it a high shelf? Barbara, look at me and tell me the truth."

"Yes very…erm, I mean no it wasn't." Barbara started to bite her nails, a sure sign she was lying.

"I think we need to talk about this later", said Olive realising that she was going to be late for church.

Leaving instructions with Geoff to pop the chicken in to the oven, Olive carefully put her furry hat on and shouted to Eileen that it was time to go. She kissed Godfrey and then turned to her husband.

"Our Barbara's got a huge bruise on her leg", she told him, "Says she did it at Ms. Butterworth's, see if she'll tell you any more about it, will you, love?"

Geoff looked startled, "You don't think that teacher's done it do you?!"

"No, don't be daft", soothed Olive, "But better we know the full story if she's had a fall."

Geoff looked doubtful, "Alright love, I'll have a chat with her."

Fastening her coat right up to the neck and making sure she had coins in her pocket for the vicar's collection plate, Olive then rushed out through the back door with Eileen hot on her heels.

Reverend Todd was apparently on holiday that week, and a temporary replacement had been sent to conduct the service. Unfortunately, Reverend Brown was on the wrong side of seventy and kept losing the thread of his sermon, causing Olive to drift off in to a reverie about her family worries. By jumping to conclusions about Barbara's teacher, Geoff had succeeded in planting a seed of suspicion in his wife's mind. It was usual for Barbara to be covered in bruises, she thought, but that was during term-time at school when she'd been tumbling around in the playground, not when she was at home. And why hadn't the old schoolmistress mentioned her pupil's fall? Olive glanced furtively over to the opposite side of the church where, three rows in front of her, Rita Butterworth sat nodding off whilst the vicar rattled off a reading. She was still dressed in grey, with a cream coloured scarf around her neck and a pretty brooch in the shape of a peacock adorning her lapel. Surely, she was nothing but a strict teacher? Olive reasoned, wouldn't she have reported any insolence to Barbara's parents before smacking the child? She could hardly believe that such a thought had even crossed her mind, it was unthinkable. Olive watched the old lady for a few minutes and then guiltily returned her focus to the aging man of the cloth.

Outside, as the congregation flocked to welcome the new priest, Olive looked around to see where Rita Butterworth was. The old lady was smiling kindly as she chatted with Mrs. Hamilton about the service, nodding her head occasionally and raising a gloved hand to acknowledge other villagers as they passed her on the threshold. Everything appeared to be quite normal with the schoolmistress and Olive chided herself for having such un-Christian thoughts as those she had entertained earlier. Therefore, feeling slightly annoyed at herself, Olive collected Eileen from Sunday school and headed up the lane towards home. Maybe Geoff had managed to get a more satisfactory answer out their daughter as to her bruising, and maybe it was nothing at all to worry about.

After eating a hearty lunch and clearing away the pots and pans, Olive questioned her husband.

"She says it was nothing" he explained, "And I'm inclined to believe her, love."

Olive nodded, it was probably nothing more than Barbara being her usual clumsy self.

Unbeknown to her parents, Barbara was having the time of her life exploring Ms. Butterworth's vast collection of books. There were fairy tales, historical dramas, classic literature and poetry, and the best part was that the schoolmistress didn't mind her pupil looking at anything that she wanted to, so long as she was careful to put it back in exactly the same place in which she found it. And it wasn't only books that the young girl was allowed to look at either. There were collections of dolls that fascinated Barbara and sometimes she was urged to take them down from their place on the shelf and examine their shiny hair and old-fashioned clothes. Of course, Barbara still had to concentrate hard on her studies but knowing that she would be allowed to spend the final fifteen minutes of her morning looking around the old lady's house made it all worthwhile.

However, there was still something about her teacher that puzzled Barbara a great deal. On her very first visit to the woman's home, Barbara had been made to promise that she would not discuss anything that she saw in the rooms. It had been impressed upon her very firmly by Ms. Butterworth that she was not to tell anyone about the books, or the dolls, or anything else. It was to be their little secret. This pleased Barbara very much. She liked knowing something that the rest of her family and friends didn't, even if it did seem like a very silly thing to have to keep to herself. Still, she kept the pact and told no-one.

That was all to change when one day Ms. Butterworth allowed Barbara to take home a second book.

The book itself wasn't an issue. It was a fairly new edition about ancient Rome and in very good condition. Barbara had pleaded with her teacher to let her borrow it overnight, as she so wanted to look at the beautiful colour pictures which depicted gladiators fighting lions, beautiful slave girls wearing strange bangles on their arms and portly Romans in togas eating grapes straight from the vine. Finally the old lady had relented but made sure that her pupil was aware that the volume should be returned the next day. This time however, she forgot to tell Barbara to keep the book hidden.

Of course Barbara was very excited and when Eileen came home from school, she dragged her sister upstairs to show her the wonderful scenes that had caused her to spend two hours poring over the book in her bedroom. Eileen was tired after a long day of study and casually picked the book up with a slight air of disinterest. She turned it over in her hands and opened the back cover. Suddenly the paper jacket fell off and something rolled out and on to the carpet. Both children screamed at the same time.

Olive raced upstairs to find both her girls standing on Eileen's bed, staring down at the flattened skeleton of a dead dormouse which lay on the carpet below.

"Oh my goodness, where on earth did that come from?"

It was Eileen who pointed to the book and nudged her sister. It wasn't long before Barbara had recounted the tale of the book's origin and then, unable to stop herself, a lot more besides. Olive was hardly able to believe what her young daughter had told her, and decided words were needed with Ms. Rita Butterworth, if only to dispel the tales of Barbara's wild imagination.

The next morning, Olive dropped her daughter off for her lessons as usual and, determining that early morning was never a good time to confront people, decided to question Rita Butterworth on her return trip at noon. Therefore, a few hours later, Olive knocked tentatively at the door of the schoolmistress's house. She waited for the customary clickety-click of shoes coming down the hallway but after a minute or so had still received no answer. As she could clearly hear jazz music being played inside, Olive turned the doorknob and peered inside. Immediately having done so, she dearly wished she hadn't.

Rita Butterworth's hallway was crammed to the rafters with books, newspapers, rotting food and empty packets. Not an inch of floor space remained, and anyone wishing to enter more than a few feet would need to climb over a mountain of rubbish to get inside and the stench of cat pee was unbearable.

"Hello", she called, "Ms. Butterworth, Barbara, are you there?" Silence.

"Helloooooo", she called again, listening carefully for a response. Somewhere further back in the house muffled voices were obviously deep in conversation.

Damn, cursed Olive, pushing Godfrey's pram into the only small space in the hallway and preparing herself to climb over the mess, she couldn't believe that she'd allowed Barbara to come here every day. Goodness, only knew what damage it could do to the poor child's lungs.

Checking that her son was sound asleep and then treading carefully over the discarded magazines and papers that leaned against piles of boxes and books, Olive began to ease her way in to the house where the voices were coming from. She could hear them more clearly now, Barbara sounding slightly afraid whilst the old lady scolded her.

"Put it back on the top shelf", came the croaky woman's voice, "It has to go back up there."

"But I can't reach Miss", complained the child, "I'm going to fall."

"Nonsense, I'm here to catch you if you do happen to slip."

"But last time I fell you didn't catch me", whined the younger voice, "And I hurt myself."

As Olive reached the door to the room from behind which she could hear the conversation, a bead of cold sweat ran down her back. It was a mother's panic telling her instinctively that something was going to happen to her child. She quickly reached for the handle and turned.

Inside the cluttered room, on top of an enormous stack of books, stood Barbara. She was red-faced and frightened, clutching a volume of 'Wind in the Willows' in one hand whilst holding on for dear life to a huge wooden bookcase with the other. Rita Butterworth stood glaring at the child with her hands on her hips and a pair of tiny round spectacles on her nose. Olive gasped.

"It's alright darling," she whispered softly to her daughter, "Give me both hands and do a big jump, just like you do when you sleep in the bunkbeds at Aunty Dolly's house."

Barbara carefully turned herself around and did as her mother instructed, dropping the book on to the floor beside her teacher in the process.

"It's alright, no need to panic..." started the old lady, bending down to pick up the novel.

"You, Ms. Butterworth are no longer employed", said Olive sternly, bustling Barbara out through the open doorway, "So I suggest you spend your retirement cleaning this disgusting pig-sty."

Rita Butterworth sniffed and picked up a scrawny tabby kitten that was looking for somewhere to poop.

"No need to be...", she muttered, but it was too late and the mother and daughter had retreated over the paper heap and back to where the oblivious baby lay snoozing.

Olive quietly closed the door and hurried away, clutching her daughter's hand tightly, and dearly wishing that it had all been a bad dream.

Chapter Seven
Jesus Crawford

Strictly speaking, Jesus Crawford was not a resident of the village. His house, a vast sprawling manor, lay on the outskirts of another community altogether but such was his involvement with the parish in which Olive and Geoff resided, there really was no question that he belonged. Of course Jesus was not his real name, but the origins of this moniker had so long been forgotten that he answered to no other and laughed alongside the children who giggled when it was called out. Even his wife, Gertrude, called him Jesus and the name did, by all accounts, suit him. It wasn't that he grew his hair long or preached religious sermons, nor did he have a group of twelve dedicated followers, but still the name was so befitting that his given name at birth was something of a distant memory. If pushed, most people would tell you that it was his sad watery eyes and long nimble fingers that caused Jesus Crawford to remind them of the Saviour. Behind closed doors, however, they would laugh and talk about his love of strappy sandals and vegetarian diet.

The Crawford's involvement with the village had come about some years before when they had happened upon a chance meeting with Reverend Todd at a local fund-raising event. Apparently the vicar had been finding it difficult to finance the multiple flower arrangements that usually adorned his church and bemoaned his woes to anyone within earshot. Luckily, for the Reverend, the Crawfords were extremely benevolent people and offered to donate a large array of floral bouquets every month, which they would deliver to the vicarage themselves on a weekly basis. Naturally the vicar was delighted with this offer and invited the couple to attend every social event on the village calendar. In time, the residents thought nothing of the Crawfords presence and gratefully accepted their kind donations to the church.

In truth, it was very easy for the villagers to warm to the couple. Jesus Crawford was a very athletic looking man, with toned limbs and a permanent tan which suggested he spent a great deal of time outdoors in his garden. He wasn't handsome at all really, but had a very kind face and sparkling eyes. His was the type of countenance that you would want to see after a tiring day at work or piece of bad fortune, and his soft mellow voice was enough to soothe any crying babe within minutes. He spoke with a slight lisp, another source of mimicry for the village youngsters, and they would take it in turns trying to engage Mr. Crawford in conversation to see how many times they could get him to say words beginning with the letter 'S'.

Gertrude Crawford, on the other hand, was physically the polar opposite of her husband. She was a very large woman, with loose folds of flesh that hung about her body like elephant hide, which she attempted to cover by wearing very colourful loose dresses but they actually did nothing for her but give the impression that she had been completely enveloped by a linen tent. Regardless of her appearance, Mrs. Crawford was just as kind as her adoring husband and sometimes you could see a smile reach the corners of her eyes before there was even a hint of humour on her lips. She had a beautiful face, despite her double chin and puffy cheeks, making it easy to imagine what an alluring female she must have been in her younger days. Now in her mid-fifties, Gertrude had almost certainly eaten herself out of shape although she still attracted side-long glances from her loving husband that clearly showed his devotion.

Olive had met the Crawfords several times and held them in high esteem. On the few occasions that she had passed their home in Geoff's car on a day out, she had been especially impressed with the high standard to which the couple maintained their gardens. Of course she had always needed to ask Geoff to slow down as they neared the Crawford residence, as it was very hard to see properly at 30mph. Besides, the garden was surrounded by a high stone wall and the only way to observe the magnificent rose bushes and perfectly manicured lawn inside was to look through the iron gates that marked the entrance. It was obvious to Olive that the couple had a great deal of money and she often found herself wondering what kind of profession Jesus Crawford had chosen. He wasn't known to work in the local town and, most times Olive had seen him, wore the type of clothing that one might feel comfortable playing tennis in. Olive knew that Mrs. Crawford didn't have children and also didn't work, neither did she need to fill her days with cooking and cleaning as it was well-known in the village that the Crawfords employed a housekeeper. So how then did Gertrude fill her days? Olive thought it must be quite a lonely life in that big house, unless the lady in question had some wonderful hobby like painting or writing poetry. Whatever she found to fill her days, Olive mused, it certainly made her happy.

In actual fact, the Crawfords really were very happy. The only bane of their existence in the countryside was the huge orchard that filled the land at the rear of their property. Not that they weren't grateful for all the fresh apples, pears and plums that kept them stocked in fresh produce all year round, but it was the orchard itself that seemed to lure the youngsters from near and far in the hope that they could bag some of the fruit for themselves when the home-owners were less than vigilant.

Year after year, the Crawfords attempted to install one deterrent after another. First it was barbed wire, but that had to be removed when some sheep from the adjoining field snagged their wool on it and became trapped. Then they had tried asking a local builder to extend the height of the wall surrounding the orchard, but he had turned out to lack the knowledge of ancient stone laying and the resulting barricade had fallen down after only a week's duration. Finally, Jesus Crawford had painted a huge white sign with red lettering, very politely telling trespassers that they would be prosecuted should they be found trying to enter, but all to no avail. It seemed that the local youths just waited until the Crawford's car left their driveway before helping themselves to whatever fruit they fancied, leaving a trail of destruction in their wake. It was the unnecessary way in which branches were broken that upset the Crawfords the most. You see, if someone had actually been brave enough to knock on their huge oak door and ask for apples, they would have been given a hearty supply and told to call again. But no, it seemed that the youngsters liked the risk of entering when they might be caught red-handed and carted off to the local police station. Jesus Crawford supposed that this was what they called fun.

Olive's first proper meeting with the Crawford's was one spring day when she had offered to take care of the flower arrangements for the church. It wasn't something that she was particularly familiar with, but several of the other ladies from the village had taken a trip to London to see the Changing of the Guard, leaving few volunteers to cover their responsibilities at the church. Always willing to help out in the community Olive had gladly offered her services and, knowing that the Crawford's usually delivered the bouquets on Friday afternoons, she had made her way down to the vicarage in plenty of time.

At the same moment that Olive reached the vicarage driveway, Jesus Crawford pulled up in his sleek bottle-green Jaguar, with Gertrude sitting beside him holding a huge bunch of lilies firmly in her hands. Olive waved and waited for them to get out.

"Hello my dear, Olive isn't it?" said Jesus Crawford cheerfully, "Lovely to see you again."

"Hello", replied Olive holding out her hand, "I hope you're both well."

"Come inside for a cup of tea with Mrs. Todd", enthused Gertrude, easing her hefty frame out of the car,

"She always has a brew waiting for us."

Olive hesitated, as she still felt a slight sensation of awkwardness when encountering the vicar and his wife. For them, it was obvious that their illicit affairs with the Hargreaves' was behind them but for Olive it had caused untold stress and embarrassment. She looked over at Gertrude Crawford who was passing the lilies to her husband and realised that life had to go on, regardless of what had happened.

Olive was ushered inside by the couple before even having time to offer her consent, and any attempt at a refusal would have been futile. Mr. and Mrs. Crawford were lovely people, so friendly and outgoing, simply bursting with positive energy. Just the kind of people she and Geoff liked to be around.

Now, Olive had heard all about Jesus and Gertrude from the other villagers, positive things of course, and was delighted to find the couple just as amiable as she had expected, having only spoken to them briefly on previous occasions. So, as Gloria Todd poured tea and handed around digestive biscuits, the little group chatted about the church and how lovely it was to be a part of such a sociable community. Olive tried her best to sound enthusiastic, but she was feeling extremely tired lately and was struggling to sleep at night. She feared that the knowledge of some of the village secrets thrust upon her was beginning to take its toll, and that included the discovery of the Reverend and Cynthia Todd's infidelity. Even more shocking had been the revelation that Stan Hargreaves had been involved. Whoever would have thought! It was very awkward sitting there drinking tea with such vivid disclosure disrupting her thoughts, but Olive persevered at light-hearted conversation until she felt that her departure could be stalled no longer. With a last parting smile, Olive gathered up the flowers from the sink where they stood in water and left the little group to continue their chinwag.

Outside she let out a sigh of relief. She had been very careful not to mention the Todd's indiscretions to any of the villagers but surely Gloria Todd must feel embarrassed in front of Olive? How could she behave as though nothing had happened between her, Reverend Todd and the Hargreaves?

It wasn't until several weeks later while out walking with Godfrey that Olive saw Jesus Crawford again. This time, he was outside the church pinning a notice to the board and stood back checking to see if it was straight. He smiled broadly as Olive approached.

"Hello Olive, who's this handsome little chap then?" he asked inquisitively, bending down to shake Godfrey's tiny hand, "Oh, I do love children, sadly Gertrude and I weren't blessed with them."

Olive tried to look sympathetic, "This is my youngest, he's just coming up to three now."

"Well, I think we might have something for him in the glove compartment", the man replied as he reached into the car, "There we go, how about a nice red apple from the tree in my garden?"

Godfrey took the apple after a little persuasion from his mother and grinned shyly.

"You really must come down and get some fruit", offered Mr. Crawford, "I'm sure with little mouths to feed you could use some. Take as much as you like. Does your husband have a car, Olive?"

Olive replied in the affirmative and said she would be delighted to take up his offer.

"Excellent, how about coming over on Saturday afternoon? I think any time after four should be alright, does that suit you."

"That would be wonderful", answered Olive, "I'll bring the girls to help pick the apples."

"Splendid, well must dash, see you Saturday. Don't forget, after four if you don't mind."

With a final wave and a pip of the horn, Jesus Crawford spun the Jaguar around and headed back down the lane away from the village, leaving Olive to look at the note that he had just pinned to the board.

"Nature Lovers are Invited to Join Us for our Summer Festival" she read aloud, "Bookings are now being taken but places are limited to twenty. First Come, First Served. Contact Duddleston Manor directly."

Olive wondered why she hadn't heard about the festival before. Strange though how they were going to limit numbers, maybe it was some very fancy soiree where the rich danced to live music and drank cocktails with names that she couldn't even pronounce. Funny how they had written 'Nature Lovers', perhaps they would be raising money for a wildlife charity or some other good cause. Olive was determined to ask the Crawfords about their festival when she collected the fruit on Saturday, maybe she could persuade Geoff to get out his best suit and take her. It was ages since they'd last had a really good night out and a party at the manor house might do them both the world of good.

As it happened, Olive didn't get chance to tell Geoff about the offer of apples or the Summer Festival that evening.

Barbara, up to her tricks again, had been playing with the local boys after school. Now that she was fully recovered from her bronchitis the child was more of a dare-devil than ever and was continually causing havoc. This particular day she had climbed a very tall oak tree on the corner of the cul-de-sac and had refused to come down. Several of the local lads had tried to climb up after her, but the little madam had filled her pockets with stones, which she had begun to hurl at the boys below, causing them to yell and make a hasty retreat. This went on for over an hour, with one young man after another attempting to scale the sides of the oak from either the side or the rear of where Barbara sat on a long branch, but each time they were driven back by a barrage of pebbles.

It wasn't until Geoff arrived home at six-thirty that Barbara realised her fun was over. However, facing her father's wrath was one thing but actually getting down from the tree was quite another. The little girl turned this way and that, trying desperately to get a foothold on the trunk while gripping the bumpy branches in her pudgy hands, but all to no avail. Climbing had been relatively easy but descending was a totally different matter, and all the while Barbara could see her father getting closer and closer as he strode over to the group of boys gathered at the foot of the oak.

"Barbara! What are you doing girl? That's no way for a young lady to behave", roared Geoff.

"I'm trying Dad", came his daughters pitiful reply as she twisted and turned on the branch.

"Stay there, I'm fetching a ladder", huffed Geoff, shaking his head and hurrying home.

By the time Geoff reached his garage, Olive had come out to see what all the commotion was about and cursed herself for not noticing what had been going on earlier. She had been so wrapped up in her baking, with the radio turned up loud, that Olive hadn't heard all the shouting and jeering going on and was now faced with a very irate husband who looked as though steam might come billowing out of his ears at any moment. He was muttering profanities under his breath and tugging the ladder from its hook on the garage wall where he kept it.

"Bloody hell mother", grumbled Geoff as he caught sight of his wife standing open mouthed on the path, "Go and fetch Billy or Bert from the farm, I'll need a hand to get that stupid child down."

Olive knew better than to say anything when Geoff was in a temper, and instead of replying she scurried off down the road in search of someone to help.

It was a good half hour later that Barbara was finally coaxed off her perch and on to the ladder and, as her feet touched the ground, the gathering crowd let out a cheer. Barbara was extremely red-faced and stomped moodily up to the house before her parents could embarrass her further by scolding her in public. No tears reached the insolent child's eyes, she was far too indignant for that, but after a serious talking to by her father and a meagre supper of just bread and butter, Barbara began to see that maybe she had pushed her luck a bit too far. As she sat sulking in her silent bedroom, the young girl's parents were downstairs eating their dinner in silence.

Every now and then, Olive glanced up to see if her husband had calmed down at all but she was met with was a frosty glare and a shake of the newspaper. It was obvious that Geoff blamed his wife for not keeping their daughter under control but, as far as Olive was concerned, the child was simply unmanageable. She was certain that every other parent in the village could allow their child to play outdoors without causing any mischief, and with the family meal to prepare how could she, as a mother, be expected to check on her children every minute she lost sight of them? After all, Barbara was unhurt and the shake up might actually keep her in order for a couple of weeks.

Eventually Olive could hold her tongue no longer and she spoke.

"There's a Summer Festival on at Duddleston Manor", she offered, "Might be nice to have a night out."

Apparently, this was the very last topic of conversation that Geoff wanted to hear.

"How the hell can we go out anywhere and leave that little rascal at home?" he fumed, "Come on, answer me that. She's a bloody nightmare."

Olive squirmed in her seat. "I just thought that perhaps…"

"No, that's your bloody trouble", grumbled Geoff, throwing his paper on the table, "You don't think, you just presume that we can swan off to some fancy gathering and nothing will happen. More than likely she'd burn the damn house down while we were away!"

"I think you might be over-reacting somewhat….." started Olive, before she was cut off.

"For Christ's sake…" but Geoff didn't finish his sentence. Instead he shrugged on his jacket and wandered outside to the garage where he had a little project to finish. Olive knew better than to follow and simply poured herself another cup of tea while she pondered how to approach Geoff about driving her to the Crawford's house to pick apples. Maybe it was best to leave that topic for another night.

Over the next few days, the tension between Olive and Geoff lifted until they were back to their old selves, laughing, joking and chatting about their daily exploits. The incident with Barbara wasn't forgotten and she was still under curfew to be home straight after school, but neither of her parents mentioned it again. The young girl knew that she had a lot of work to do, both physically and emotionally, before she would be completely forgiven, but at least for now the worst punishment she would receive was a few days stuck in the house under her mother's watchful eye.

By the weekend, the household was almost back to its usual routine and everyone looked forward to the visitors that were expected on Sunday. Olive had received a letter from her younger sister Minnie, saying that her husband Ron would be bringing her over for the day, as she had some news to share with her. Olive knew that Minnie must be pregnant, why else would she want to share her news in person? After all, the upbeat tone of her sibling's letter had suggested that Minnie was bubbling with happiness and Olive couldn't wait to start the celebrations.

On Friday, with the girls at school and Mrs. Hamilton kindly offering to take care of Godfrey for a few hours, Olive caught the bus in to town to buy some linen napkins. It wasn't that she wanted to show off to her younger sister, but she did want the table to look perfect for their family gathering and smart new napkins were just the thing to add a splash of colour to Olive's white China crockery.

After making her purchase at the huge department store, Olive decided to treat herself to a cup of coffee in the market square café before having another little wander around the shops. She still had two hours before catching the return bus home, and intended to make the most of this rare opportunity of being child-free, something that only usually happened when she attended church on Sundays.

As she sat in a window seat with a cup of freshly brewed coffee and a custard slice in front of her, Olive took in the buildings outside. A delightful mix of Edwardian grey granite and Tudor architecture, the town was a bustling hive of activity. Market stalls were set up all around the pedestrian area and local produce was traded freely. There was a butcher selling his prized pork sausages, a lady selling beautiful knitwear, the Women's Institute stall covered with jams and preserves, freshly cut flowers arranged in huge tubs and a wonderful display of fruit and vegetables, polished and gleaming in the sunlight.

Suddenly Olive jumped. Two faces had appeared at the window and were waving at her through the glass. She instantly recognised the Crawfords and raised her hand in acknowledgement, half expecting them to continue their shopping in the square. However, the couple had other ideas and rushed in to the cafe looking excited and headed straight for Olive's table, pulling up chairs as they neared her.

"Do you mind very much if we join you?" gushed Gertrude, already dropping her bags next to Olive's chair and taking off her multi-coloured chiffon scarf.

"No, of course not…" smiled Olive, moving her own chair over to make more room.

"Wonderful", chirped Jesus Crawford, setting his huge hands on the table, "Lovely to see you."

The waitress appeared and took their order, an iced tea and oatcake for Gertrude while her husband opted for a milky coffee and a large slice of chocolate cake. Olive suppressed a smile, if she'd had to lay a bet on who would have ordered what, she would definitely have lost.

"So, what brings you into town…" questioned Gertrude, leaning closely towards Olive's face.

Olive briefly explained her purchase and listened as her companions told her about their own bags of shopping, which were brimming with all matter of household goods. During the amiable conversation, refreshments were served and he waitress bustled around trying to fit everything on to the table. Suddenly Olive remembered about the Crawford's Summer Festival thinking that, if she just went ahead and arranged everything, Geoff might be persuaded to have an evening out.

"I meant to ask…" she ventured, "Do you have any seats available for your little soiree?"

The couple shot each other such a strange look, almost of surprise that Olive had asked, but it was Jesus who broke the news that sadly the event was already fully booked.

"Oh, what a pity", Olive replied, genuinely disappointed, "I knew I should have booked it right away."

"Well, we didn't realise it was your type of thing", faltered Gertrude, "With it being a nature event."

"Oh, I love everything to do with wildlife and the country", gushed Olive, "But never mind."

The odd look passed between Mrs. Crawford and her husband again, but this time they simply stayed quiet and busied themselves with tucking in to their respective desserts.

Sensing that the conversation had come to an abrupt end, Olive said that she must be getting home soon and waved at the waitress for the bill. The young girl was quick to walk over.

"Wish we could offer you a lift my dear", frowned Jesus Crawford, "But I'm afraid that our motor car only has two seats, hardly enough room for Gertrude and the shopping."

"Don't be silly", Olive replied, counting out coins from her purse, "I'll be fine on the bus."

"Let me at least pay for your coffee", enthused the tall man, pushing a note at the waitress before Olive could protest, "And we'll see you tomorrow for some apples. After four alright?"

"Thank you for the coffee. That's very kind", smiled Olive, "I'll see you tomorrow then."

With that, feeling as though something unsaid between Mr and Mrs Crawford meant a lot more than they had ventured to tell, Olive made her way to the bus-stop, calling only at the bakery for a loaf.

On Saturday morning Olive set off to the village shop to purchase the things that she needed to cook a sumptuous feast for her sister and brother-in-law. She knew from past lunches that Minnie and Ron both enjoyed her cooking and she looked forward to displaying her talent with relish. Of course Geoff was always very complimentary of everything that Olive set before him on the dinner table, but when cooking for guests she always liked to make an extra special effort.

As she walked down the lane in the early sunshine, with Godfrey on one side and her girls carrying a wicker basket on the other, Olive made a mental note of all the things that she would require. She had already counted out the cutlery and plates, and had ironed the creases out of the new napkins, which Geoff had commented on as a complete and utter waste of time. Olive hadn't retorted as she normally would have, but smiled pleasantly whilst at the same time taking no notice. As she walked in the early morning sunshine with her children, Olive went through the menu in her head. They had a big juicy chicken in the larder, which Geoff had fetched earlier from the farm, and an abundance of home-grown vegetables from their own back garden, so there would only be the need to buy sugar and flour for the apple pie.

"Apples!" exclaimed Olive, as she suddenly realised that today was Saturday, the day which she had arranged to pick apples from Jesus Crawford's orchard. All three children looked curiously at their mother, and she was obliged to explain herself. Barbara was especially delighted at the prospect of picking apples that afternoon, that was until Olive explained that there would be no tree-climbing involved whatsoever. After returning home with their goods, the children went off to follow their various pursuits while Olive went in to the back garden to find Geoff, who was busily tying some runner beans to a pole. She quickly recounted her conversation with Mr. Crawford, and smiled at Geoff as she asked him to drive to the manor house that afternoon. He was more than happy to oblige he said, no problem at all, but he would have to be home by four as he'd promised to meet his boss to go over some new contracts.

Olive remembered what Jesus Crawford had said about not going before four o'clock, but he'd been smiling she recalled and surely wouldn't mind if they went an hour early. Would he?

Therefore at three, with the children sitting safely in the back and Olive next to him, Geoff reversed the Austin off the drive and headed down the road towards Duddleston Manor. Everyone was in good spirits and the family sang some popular tunes as they rode through open countryside.

On arrival, Olive said it might be best if she checked with the Crawfords before getting the children out of the car, just in case there was a problem with them arriving early, so she wandered up to the huge front door by herself and rang the doorbell. Olive could hear the sound of the bell echoing around the house, but as she waited for a few minutes, no footsteps could be heard coming to answer the door. Maybe the couple were out, she wondered. Olive hesitated for a moment deciding what to do, and then slowly craned her neck to casually peer through the side window. Nothing. All she could see was a vast expanse of highly polished wooden floor, which ended in a palatial staircase at the end of the hallway. Huge oil paintings hung on either side of the walls but Olive wasn't close enough to determine whether they were portrait, landscape or some new-fangled type of modern art. All of a sudden she heard the sound of laughter coming from the back garden which was out of view and obviously located at the far side of the manor. Carefully she walked across the pebbled path, treading carefully in her open-toe sandals, in search of the people whose voices she could now hear quite clearly, Olive kept close to the house until a tennis court came in to view. There were high nets on all sides with a mesh doorway installed on one side.

The sight that now befell Olive's eyes was quite a shock.

Jesus and Gertrude Crawford were both completely naked, prancing around the court with their tennis racquets waving as they volleyed the ball backwards and forwards. Both were enjoying themselves so much that they didn't notice their alarmed guest staring from the sidelines. Olive gasped as she took in the scene. Gertrude's rolls of ghostly white stomach fat wobbled like some uncontrollable blancmange and Jesus Crawford's tiny manhood swung to and fro like a yo-yo. The couple seemed to be having immense fun and acted as though being without clothes was the most natural thing in the world. As she stood there, deciding whether she could run back to the car without the Crawfords seeing her, Olive now noticed another couple, the man apparently acting as umpire and the woman cutting up oranges on a small patio table. This pair were also baring their flesh in a most brash manner, the man sitting with his legs apart as he called out each time a player hit the ball outside of the lines and the woman stretching her arms above her head every now and again revealing dark hairy armpits.

Olive stepped backwards slowly, realising that if she made another move now they would hear her sandals crunching on the gravel. She was mortified at the thought that any moment one of the four nudists might turn their gaze towards her. Gently she slipped off her footwear and tip-toed over the stones until she had turned the corner of the manor house wall, where she then ran towards the car as fast as her feet would carry her. She arrived flustered and out of breath.

"Can we get the apples now Mum?" asked Eileen, who had been waiting patiently, "What about the pie?"

"No", Olive managed to say through gritted teeth, "Not today, love. Definitely not today."

"Why aren't you wearing your shoes?" asked Geoff, looking startled, "What happened?."

Olive glanced at the children in the back seat, "No reason. Erm, girls, the Crawfords weren't at home."

Geoff was most astute when it came to his wife telling little white lies and concluded that it would be best to question her back at home when the children were occupied with their various games. He steered the car home in silence, now and again looking across at Olive's pale face, worried that she might be about to deposit her lunch all over his smart leather interior. As soon as they got home, Olive reached for two aspirin from the cupboard and gulped them down with a glass of cold water. Geoff followed her to the sink and waited for her to speak, expecting her to either say that she had been chased by a very large dog or propositioned by the Crawford's elderly gardener.

"I've never seen anything like it in my life…" Olive began, shaking her head, 'Oh, Good Lord Geoff."

Geoff was about to enquire further but when he looked up a long black car had pulled up outside and the familiar figure of his boss, Mr. Higginbotham, jumped out stretching his short fat legs as he did so.

"We'll talk about this later, love", said Geoff awkwardly stepping towards the door, "Put your feet up and have a cuppa, I promise I won't be more than an hour."

Olive nodded, that was Geoff's answer to all life's dramas she mused, have a bloody cup of tea.

It was actually three hours later that Geoff returned home, having stopped for a bite to eat at a tavern in town with his boss. By that time Olive wasn't upset or angry, she was just feeling very confused.

"Blimey", coughed Geoff, after hearing the sequence of events told to him by his wife, "And you never suspected a thing?" Olive shook her head, quite unable to say any more on the subject. Geoff gave her a bear hug and stroked her hair. "It's alright, leave the silly bugger's to it, that's what I say."

Olive nodded, Geoff was probably right, after all the Crawfords had been on their own property.

She scooped cocoa in to two enamel mugs and began heating up some milk as her husband continued.

"I wonder if Mr. Higginbotham knows what they get up to", he chuckled.

Olive turned around sharply, "It's not funny Geoff. Why would he know the Crawfords?"

"His wife plays tennis with Gertrude Crawford", Geoff explained, "She's always over at the Manor."

Olive began to speak but stopped, thoughts running wild in her mind, surely it couldn't be?

Two seconds later, Geoff confirmed her worst fears.

"Old Higginbotham dropped her off there earlier today as a matter of fact."

The couple faced each other, stumped by their joint realisation. Of one thing they were certain, Geoff was going to have trouble looking his boss in the eye on Monday morning!

Chapter Eight
Elsie Corbett

For several weeks after the manor house incident, Olive was inclined to distance herself from the rest of the villagers and even suggested to Geoff that they spend a few Sundays visiting relatives instead of the usual ritual of going to church. She was flustered and shocked, the past couple of years living in the countryside had really opened Olive's eyes and she wasn't sure how many more revelations she could take. Sleep deprivation and nightmares alternately invaded her nights and during the day she felt lethargic and emotional. Geoff had laughed when she had first described the scene of naked middle-aged couples prancing around a tennis court and although he could see that his wife was deeply shocked by the shenanigans, he was of the opinion that folk had a right to behave how they liked on their own land, whether it be with their clothes on or without.

Gradually the raucous sight faded from Olive's memory and she endeavoured to fall back in to her daily routine. Of course she had missed the church services, but even those hadn't been quite the same since she had found out about the Reverend's escapades. Life in the village really was becoming complex.

Olive was deliberating about her family's future in the village, wondering if they should move but then worrying about finding another house that was close enough for the children to travel to the same schools. It would be upheaval enough, if she did manage to persuade Geoff to move house, without the children having to find new friends as well. Olive had spoken to all three of her sisters about the antics of the villagers but their reactions had all been the same. Why move from such a wonderful location for the sake of a few sordid secrets, they had asked, another such perfect cottage might not be found for miles. Stay put, they had urged, at least for another summer.

Olive wondered if she found a new hobby that it might take her mind off things. She had always been a very good cook and thought she might like to try her hand at cake-decorating. There were always birthdays or anniversaries to celebrate, perhaps she could even make some extra money by selling her confectionary locally. Geoff thought it was a wonderful idea, and made sure that his wife had extra house-keeping money to buy all the ingredients that she would need. He had no idea whether this new interest was just a passing phase, or would turn into something lucrative, but he was delighted to see Olive with a spring in her step again and encouraged her to join a class at the village hall. After a couple of weeks, Olive was making such good progress that the mother of one of Eileen's friends had asked her to make a cake for the child's upcoming birthday. Nothing fancy, just a pale pink cake decorated with fondant roses and the name iced on to the top, and it was well within Olive's capabilities.

She had two weeks to showcase her new found skills, and Olive was extremely excited. She had carefully calculated the cost, with just a little extra for her time, which had been readily agreed by the girl's mother. And so, with a task at hand and a passion for creativity Olive began planning the cake.

Naturally, the first thing to do was buy the ingredients, some of which would need to be ordered from the village shop as they seldom kept items such as icing sugar and food colouring in stock. She had opted for a chocolate cake, knowing how much her own children enjoyed the taste of rich dark sponge, even though it was bound to cause extra washing of clothes and sticky faces when they'd finished. Olive knew it would be a hit with the children at the birthday party and felt a sense of anticipation as she imagined the first moment when her wonderful creation would be revealed for the first time. As soon as her first order had arrived, Olive had begun to prepare her shopping list.

Elsie Corbett was the elderly shopkeeper that kept the village stores. When her husband had passed away a decade before, she had considered retiring but as her only son had emigrated to Canada, Elsie had no idea how she would keep herself occupied if she wasn't standing behind the shop counter. She wasn't an advocate for change either, much to the annoyance of some of the locals. Over the years, people had made suggestions about adding new products to the stock, perhaps updating the cash register or maybe hiring a young man to help with the more strenuous tasks of running a business, but Elsie had solemnly shook her head. No, she had said, she would run her little business the same as she always had, which was in the same manner as that of her father before her. Sometimes Elsie Corbett's 'way' was a little frustrating, especially when she insisted on calculating a person's bill on a scrap of paper instead of ringing each item through the till. On occasions there had been a queue of half a dozen customers waiting to be served while she checked and double-checked the prices of each article.

The villagers were patient folks as a whole, and chatted casually as they waited in line. Strangers passing through weren't always so forgiving, and would huff and puff as the old lady hunched over her figures almost as if her very life depended upon it. One thing that could be admired about Elsie's shop was the cleanliness. Every item stood upright upon a sparkling shelf, labelling facing clearly to the front and not a spot of dust or cobweb to be seen anywhere. There had been more than a few occasions when people had cause to question the age of some of the stock, but Elsie had also been quick to reply, "What do you expect if I don't sell very many of that particular brand or item." The villagers were always satisfied with the old woman's answer, after all, not everyone drank the same brand of tea or liked the same biscuits, so it was inevitable that sometimes things would reach their sell by date whilst sitting upon the shelves of the village store.

If truth be told, very few dared to argue with Elsie Corbett either, and accepted her explanation rather than feel the wrath of her very sharp and sarcastic tongue.

She was a short woman of small proportions with soft grey curly hair and tiny features. Her eyes were a chocolate brown and betrayed a hidden youthfulness beneath a slightly wrinkled exterior. Elsie's everyday work attire consisted of a white overall over the top of a plain dark dress, her stockings always seemed to look a little bit loose over her sparrow-like legs and puckered in soft folds around her ankles. Her family had owned the shop for four generations and had lived above it regardless of how large, or small, their family happened to be. Elsie Corbett's own family had consisted of three, her husband and son being the other two. Much to her dismay her only child had flown the nest on his twenty-first birthday, taking a job with a news agency in Canada. Of course the Corbett's had been very proud of their boy but also felt bitter disappointment that he hadn't wanted to stay in the village and take over the family business that would be rightfully his someday. When Elsie's husband had died from a heart attack years later, the prodigal son had dutifully returned home for the funeral but departed again two days later, never to be seen again. Of course he wrote to his mother on a monthly basis but the distance had caused a rift and the letters became shorter and shorter until now, twenty years after leaving the village, Elsie received just a short update of her son's life and the occasional photograph of his own family.

Olive quite liked Elsie Corbett's straight-talking no-nonsense attitude and the respect was mutual. Elsie admired the ease with which Olive and Geoff had integrated their family in to village life, although Elsie had, on a couple of occasions, taken their youngest daughter to one side and issued a word of warning for being insolent and rowdy. The girl's parents would never find out from the shopkeeper's lips though, as Elsie felt it sufficient to keep her own watchful eye on the little rascal, certainly there was no harm done if the child simply learned to mind her manners.

Armed with a list of half a dozen ingredients, Olive stepped over the doorstep of the village shop, stopping momentarily to look up at the little brass bell tinkling softly overhead, and made her way to the polished counter. Elsie was standing with her back to the door, dressed in a crisp white apron, busily dusting the huge jars of sweets that lined the wooden shelves at the rear of the shop. They were strategically placed, just out of the reach of children, but not so high as to be beyond the grasp of an average height adult. Olive smiled, it was almost as though Elsie Corbett's family had spent their lives moving goods and building shelves, everything was so well organised. She gave a little cough, which forced Elsie to turn around to face her customer.

"Hello dear, it's a cold morning isn't it? Now, what can I get you?"

Olive pushed her list forward, "I need these items please", she said politely, "I'm making a special birthday cake for one of the children's friends."

The old woman slid the piece of paper across the counter towards her and shook her head slowly.

"I can't get you any icing sugar or candles until Friday morning I'm afraid Olive, but luckily the rest of the things are in stock."

Olive thought for a moment, if she made the cake on Thursday and decorated it on Friday there would still be plenty of time for her to put the finishing touches to it before Geoff delivered it on Saturday afternoon.

"That will be fine", she concluded.

"I'll just have to pop into the stockroom to get you a large tub of cocoa", Elsie muttered as she pushed her way through a beaded curtain, "We only usually sell the smaller ones, but I'm sure I've got a large one."

"No hurry", shouted Olive as the old lady disappeared, "I'll just have a look around."

It was over five minutes before the shopkeeper appeared again, during which time Olive had perused the goods on display and peeked at the headlines on the cover of the daily newspaper. She found it quite amusing that the shop contained the type of goods which Elsie 'thought' her customers would want but actually held a huge amount of stock that could seldom be of use. Olive noted the packets of powdered eggs, a necessity during the war years but now worthless here in the country where chickens were plentiful. There were various herbal remedies lining another shelf, claiming cures for everything from stomach ailments to earache, but the labels had become faded and brown.

"Here we are", announced Elsie Corbett, holding a large tub of cocoa powder in her gnarled fingers, "Now then, what's next on your list?"

And so the process went on, item after item being slowly produced until the only missing articles were those which had been discussed earlier. Olive lifted the goods into her basket one by one as the old woman wrote down the prices in her illegible scrawl, and suddenly noticed that the bag of flour had a piece of tape securing its top flap. It also didn't feel as full as she would have expected.

"Oh, I think there may be something wrong with this", Olive pointed out, "It seems to have been opened."

"Nonsense", laughed Elsie, "Sometimes I do quality checks, that's all. I tape them straight back up after taking a little sample." Olive wasn't convinced, wasn't that the job of the manufacturers?

Still, she didn't want to upset the old widow and put the bag of flour into her basket.

That Thursday, Olive put the girls on the bus to school and set about creating her first commissioned cake. Her sister had offered to look after Godfrey for a couple of days, giving Olive the freedom to spend as much time as she needed baking, decorating and perfecting. She had already decided to put her personal touch on the cake and had spent several evenings creating perfect fondant roses in various shades of pink and white. For these, she had made a special journey in to town for the fondant but knew that her special effort would be rewarded once word of her creation had built her a reputation.

As Olive took out her mixing bowl and weighing scales, she struggled to think of anything that she would rather be doing right at that moment, and hoped that her destiny lay in providing sweet temptations for others. As she fell in to a daydream about her culinary future, Olive reached into the cupboard for the flour and started to carefully pour it into the bowl of the weighing scales. Before reaching the required measurement, however, the bag had become empty.

"That's funny", murmured Olive, "There should have been two pounds of flour exactly, and I'm fifty grams short." She tipped the contents in to her mixing bowl and began the process of weighing out the flour again, scooping it back on to the weighing apparatus with a large spoon, so as not to spill any. Still the result was the same, fifty grams of flour was missing. Olive tentatively touched the top of the paper bag, remembering what Elsie Corbett had said about checking the quality. How much had the old woman taken out? All fifty grams? And how would a rural shopkeeper conduct a quality check on flour?

Needing to finish her baking in order to let the cake cool overnight, Olive had no choice but to return to the village shop for another bag of flour. This time the old woman was busy serving Mrs. Muller and failed to notice Olive peering closely at the bags of flour on the shelf.

'Well, these ones all seem to be sealed properly', thought Olive, 'Perhaps it was just that one bag'. She stood deliberating for a few seconds, should she raise her concerns and risk upsetting the aged shopkeeper or say nothing and just purchase another replacement bag of flour.

"I tell you, several of these biscuits were missing."

Olive turned sharply to catch Anna Muller's hushed voice insistently pressing the shopkeeper.

"That's impossible", replied Elsie Corbett sharply, "You must be mistaken."

The tall Russian stiffened. She was never purposely a confrontational person and decided that perhaps this conversation was best forgotten. She slowly picked up the packet of custard creams that lay on the polished counter between her and the old woman, and bade both women good day.

"What was all that about?' asked Olive inquisitively, "Is there a problem with something?"

"Nothing at all", responded the old lady abruptly, "Now, just the flour was it Olive?"

She nodded, realising that Elsie Corbett had become flustered and defensive. Olive smiled and asked if everything was alright with the old lady.

"Oh, don't worry about me", Elsie scoffed, "You get those difficult customers sometimes."

Olive attempted to show a sympathetic face but found it very difficult. She knew that Anna Muller was probably the very least confrontational of all the villagers and wouldn't complain without reason.

"Shall I make us a cup of tea?"

Olive was startled at the unexpected offer of a brew, but found herself feeling compassion for Elsie Corbett and agreed to stay just long enough to enjoy a quick drink. Maybe the shopkeeper was lonely and needed some company for a while, she thought, it would do no harm to stop and chat for a while. And so, a few minutes later, with china teacups in their hands the two women entered into their first proper conversation since Olive's arrival in the village.

"You've got a lovely young family", started Elsie, "And such a smart and hard-working husband."

Olive blushed, "Yes, I'm very proud of them", she replied, blowing on her tea to cool it slightly.

"It's a wonder those neighbours of yours haven't had any children yet", Elsie continued, "They must have been married for a fair few years now don't you think?"

Olive nodded politely but said nothing. She had no intention of getting in to a debate over what the Muller's did or didn't do, especially after the conversation that she'd overheard all that time ago. Instead, she made an attempt to steer the conversation back to a much more general topic.

"Have you been busy this morning?" she asked, "You must get a lot of customers near the weekend."

"Oh, no more than usual", Elsie shrugged, seeming quite genuinely surprised that Olive was taking such an interest in shop business,

"You'd be amazed at the number of folks who do their weekly shop and then come back in an hour later for something they'd forgotten to buy."

Olive wondered how many people had also returned with a complaint of some sort or another.

"Had Anna Muller forgotten something?" Olive ventured, "She seemed a bit flustered."

"No, that was something else entirely", whispered Elsie leaning closer, "She brought back a packet of biscuits that she'd already opened. These foreigners are such strange people."

Olive decided it was best to say nothing more regarding the incident and, looking at the clock above the counter, she slid off her stool and explained that it was time she went on her way.

"It's been lovely chatting with you", smiled Elsie, "See you tomorrow for the icing sugar."

As Olive returned home and continued to make the cake, she couldn't help thinking about the strange incident at the shop. If she wasn't mistaken, Mrs. Muller had seemed to be complaining about missing biscuits. What a coincidence, had they also been sealed with a small square of tape? As she whisked and creamed, Olive considered the awful possibility that Elsie Corbett might be trying to conceal the presence of rats in her storeroom. After all, it wasn't unheard of, especially in the countryside.

The following morning, Olive was up bright and early, ready to collect her icing sugar and birthday candles from the village shop. Being something of an amateur sleuth at heart, she had already decided to look for further evidence of opened packets or anything else that may have been tampered with on the shelves of the local store. As luck would have it, there were already a couple of customers getting their early morning newspaper and loaves of bread, and Olive had chance to discreetly look at the goods on display. As her eyes scanned carefully, Olive found more than a few items of food with tape sealing the edges, tins of tea, jars of jam and even a box of breakfast cereal all showed signs of having been previously opened. The boxes Olive could understand, as a rodent might be able to nibble its way through a corner of the cardboard packaging, but who ever heard of a rat that could open a jar of preserves? Olive was very confused. Something was going on here, and she dearly wished she had never discovered it. Maybe it would be best if Geoff came to offer his services as chief rat-catcher, she pondered.

"Hello, dear. Time for a quick cuppa?" Elsie enquired, "I've got some nice jam tarts in the back."

"Alright, you've twisted my arm", laughed Olive, "But I really can't stay long."

The shop-keeper wandered in to the back room to prepare the drinks while Olive made herself comfortable on one of the high wooden stools at the end of the counter. Minutes later Elsie had returned with the refreshments and started to tell Olive about her busy morning serving customers.

"Mrs. Todd came in at nine o'clock sharp", began the woman, "Said she needed some soap. I mean who needs soap so urgently at that time in a morning..?"

Fortunately, this rendition was interrupted by a steady flow of villagers entering the shop to buy various everyday items such as peppermints, dried fruit and coffee. Olive watched as Elsie advised her patrons on the merits of one brand versus another, amused that it always seemed to be the most expensive product that the shopkeeper recommended for purchase.

"Now where were we...?" chattered Elsie, having satisfied her customers and returned to her stool.

Olive was just about to speak when the little bell tinkled again and her neighbour entered the shop.

"Good morning ladies", chirped Mrs. Hamilton, "What a very fine day it is."

The two other women smiled and said hello, waiting for Mrs. Hamilton to close the door and make her way over to the counter where they sat finishing off the jam tarts.

"I've got your magazine right here", muttered Elsie, reaching down to a hidden shelf under the counter, "There are some lovely knitting patterns and recipes this week." She paused, realising that both Olive and Mrs. Hamilton must be supposing that she had read the magazine cover to cover.

"Ooh, I hope you don't think that I..." she faltered, feeling a warm heat rise up to her cheeks.

Mrs. Hamilton laughed, "Don't be silly Elsie. Of course not."

The shopkeeper breathed deeply through her nose. "Was there anything else?'?

"Now that you come to mention it..." Olive's neighbour remarked, reaching to the bottom of her small wicker basket, "I bought these crackers yesterday, but they're not sealed properly."

Elsie blushed again and took the package, which she placed to one side. She then silently walked over to where the stock of water biscuits resided on a shelf and took a fresh packet.

"Here you go", she said indignantly handing it over and glancing in Olive's direction, "We've had a lot of complaints about that brand. I certainly won't be stocking them again."

Mrs. Hamilton thanked the older woman and counted out the money for her magazine.

"Well, I'd better get back", she said, "The house doesn't clean itself."

Olive pulled her coat closed and picked up her bag of icing sugar, "I'll walk back with you."

As the two ladies sauntered up the lane towards the cul-de-sac, Mrs. Hamilton smiled at Olive and gave her a little nudge. "You're getting on well with old Elsie Corbett these days."

Olive sighed. "I think she's a bit lonely, I've only really chatted to her a couple of times."

"I'm jesting dear", giggled her neighbour, "Although keep an eye on what you're buying from her, she has a tendency to open packets for one reason or another."

Olive didn't reply straight away, instead she contemplated the idea of explaining about her theory of the rat-infested stockroom but immediately thought better of it, for Elsie's sake.

"Alright", she said at last, "I'll keep an eye open."

Olive really wanted to discuss the situation with Mrs. Hamilton, after all she was beginning to think that she was actually one of the very few sane people who resided in the village, but a sense of duty to the old lady at the shop won out and she kept her mouth firmly closed. After all, once she had explained the circumstances to her husband, they might be able to help Elsie Corbett save face.

That evening, with her master-piece iced and dinner on the table, Olive recounted her experiences at the shop over the past few days. Geoff was very reluctant to get involved but eventually agreed that it was a man's job to help out, if indeed the old lady had an infestation of some kind.

"I suppose I could offer to lay some traps for her", he tutted, "Blimey, is my work ever done?"

"Don't be like that", chided Olive, "You'd be helping an old lady, I don't think she has any family."

"Alright, alright, no need to make me feel guilty", laughed Geoff, "If it means we can get a full packet of cornflakes in a morning, I'll do it."

Olive was satisfied that this would be an end to the curiosity, once Elsie Corbett was rid of the rodents, she would have no need to spend time sealing up the packets. It made Olive shiver to think that she might have been sharing her groceries with vermin but she also understood that the old lady probably couldn't afford to throw away large quantities of stock either.

The next day Geoff filled a sack with traps that he'd bought at a hardware store on his way back from the foundry and set off for the shop five minutes before closing time. Elsie Corbett was alone and just about to empty the cash register. Geoff gently explained his reason for being there, emphasising his wife's concern that there may be something nibbling at the food in the stockroom. At first the old woman just looked at him blankly and Geoff felt the heat of embarrassment rising up his neck. Then, all of a sudden, it was as if a light switched on in the shopkeeper's head and she seemed to understand.

"Oh, the packets! Oh, yes, perhaps there is something in the storeroom, thank you Geoff."

She lifted up the counter hatch and led him through the beaded curtains to the rear of the shop. Everything seemed clean and neat, nothing out of the ordinary. Except, Geoff suddenly realised, there was no stock whatsoever on the floor, so the little devils must be climbing up the metal racking to get to the food! He'd soon put paid to that, he thought, and got down on his hands and knees to start placing the traps in each corner of the room and next to the small holes in the skirting board. Elsie watched the process in silence, but seemed happy enough that someone had come to assist. After laying the last contraption, Geoff scrambled to his feet and brushed his trousers.

"I'll come back tomorrow to see if we've caught anything", he promised.

Elsie Corbett said nothing at first, simply eyeing him carefully and looking around the floor at the traps.

"Thank you", she finally whispered, closing the shop door and turning the sign over as Geoff left.

He could still feel the old woman's eyes peering at him as he made his way back up the lane and wondered if she'd been embarrassed that Olive had noticed the presence of rats in the shop. Geoff glanced back over his shoulder and caught sight of Mrs. Corbett standing behind the glass panel in the shop door with the 'Closed' sign still in her hand. He raised a hand in acknowledgement but the old lady hurriedly retreated back towards the stockroom and ignored his gesture. Funny woman, he thought.

"Everything sorted?" Olive enquired as Geoff entered the house, "Was she okay with you?"

"Not sure really", Geoff replied, "Couldn't see any evidence of rats to be honest, love, but I'll go back in the morning and see if there's anything in the traps."

Olive stroked his back. She had a good husband, always willing to help others and a wonderful father.

The next morning Olive had risen early to put the finishing touches to the birthday cake, and proudly displayed it on the work surface for her family to see as they entered the kitchen for breakfast.

"Wow! That's wonderful", cooed Barbara and Eileen, "Can you eat the flowers?"

Their mother nodded in the affirmative, "I'm going to make you both a cake like this for your birthdays."

"Not for me", replied Barbara, wrinkling up her nose, "I want a cake with fishes on it!"

Olive, Eileen and Geoff burst in to laughter, Barbara was such a tomboy, her latest hobby had been to go fishing with Olive's brothers so no wonder she had requested such a strange theme for her cake.

"I'm off to collect those T..R..A..P..S.." Geoff whispered quietly to Olive, hiding a hessian sack behind his back so as not to alert the children to his plans.

"What traps?" snapped the girls in unison.

Olive giggled, there was certainly nothing wrong with either of their spelling capabilities.

Geoff simply shook his head and left their mother to explain while he set off for the village shop.

Suddenly Olive raced down the drive behind him, arms flapping as she tried to grab his attention.

"Go around the back", she cautioned, "It wouldn't be fair if any of the customers caught wind of vermin in the shop would it? And be sympathetic towards Mrs. Corbett if you do find something."

Geoff loved his wife dearly but sometimes wished she would give him more credit when it came to being tactful. Of course he was planning to go around the back he told her, and of course he would break the news as carefully as he could. Shaking his head in disbelief, Geoff set off again on his walk.

The side of the shop ran parallel to a small hedgerow which bordered a field full of sheep, obscuring any visitors from immediate observation, so Geoff was easily able to walk around the back to the stockroom without being seen by anyone standing near the shop window. He felt a bit like some dastardly villain going on a secret mission, sneaking in to the cold store in search of hungry rodents, but he realised that the quieter he could be, the more likely he would be able to catch something chewing away on some of the food. It made his skin crawl just thinking about what he might find but he'd promised Olive that he would see to it and he'd do anything just for a quiet life.

He opened the door as slowly as possible, making sure that the creaky old handle didn't make too much noise as he lifted it back into its neutral position. From what he could see so far, the traps were all empty and there was no sign that anything had been feasting in the night. Geoff could hear a rustling noise coming from behind the beaded curtain however, and tiptoed over to see what was there. Something or somebody was definitely eating but it sounded much large than a rat.

As he crept closer, Geoff could clearly see Elsie Corbett seated at the counter in her familiar white apron, with a cup of tea in one hand and a packet of chocolate bourbons in the other. He was just about to speak when he noticed a roll of tape lying on the counter next to her. Was this just some strange coincidence, he wondered. Geoff continued to watch from his veiled vantage point, feeling guilty that he was sneaking around and wondering how he would explain himself should the little shopkeeper suddenly turn around, but as he stood transfixed, everything suddenly became clear.

Elsie Corbett removed three biscuits from the small brown bourbon packet and examined them carefully, as though deciding whether to eat them or return them to the pack. Obviously electing to consume them, she carefully folded over the ends of the open wrapper into a neat envelope-like shape, and then took a piece of tape and carefully secured the open end tightly until nothing could fall out. Then the old woman nimbly jumped off her stool and wandered over to the shelf where other identical, but full, packets were all lined up together. With her left hand the shopkeeper pulled three packets of bourbon biscuits towards the front and with her right hand deftly inserted the opened packet in to the space. She then pushed the other packets back in place and turned her attention to a pile of women's magazines.

Geoff stood transfixed. So there were no rats after all. He took three paces back towards the door and opened it loudly, enabling the old lady to hear him entering.

"Just come to get the traps", he shouted, "Seems you're rodent free though Elsie."

"Oh well, never mind", the old lady shouted, "They must have gone away. Thank you Geoff."

Geoff gathered up the traps, dropping them deftly in to the hessian sack and left without saying much more. Elsie Corbett was too engrossed in reading a women's magazine that one of her customer's had ordered to notice the look of utter disbelief on the man's face and she did little more than raise her head slightly when she heard the click of the door as Geoff let himself out and trudged back up the lane.

Goodness me, he thought, I'll have a good deal to tell Olive over a cup of tea at home.

Chapter Nine
The Walkers

As spring turned to summer, Geoff began to settle in to a new routine at the foundry. Work was steady and new staff had been employed, which now offered him the flexibility of starting earlier in the mornings and setting off home an hour earlier in the evenings.

Now that baby Godfrey was starting to notice the exciting world around him, Geoff decided to use this extra time taking his son on a tour around the village. Together they explored the hedgerows, saw wild animals frolicking in the fields and used the time to catch up with the other villagers. Geoff had never been one for idle gossip, but he was more than happy to while away some time chatting about the weather or the latest events taking place at the village hall.

Of course Olive was delighted with this new turn of events as it meant she could have some time to herself in the evenings. With Eileen and Barbara settled at the table doing homework, Olive could run a hot bath and relax, or sit on the sofa and knit to her hearts content without having to worry about her young son. She was also very pleased that Geoff and Godfrey were having some time alone together, and she hoped that in a few years her husband would use the time to teach his boy to fish, make things out of wood and do random jobs such as changing a bicycle tyre or mowing the lawn.

Every evening after tea, weather permitting, father and son would set off on their walk, turning in a different direction or unexplored lane each time, until all the roads and pathways to the village had been traversed and then they started all over again. One such lane, to the left of the cul-de-sac in which the family lived, led uphill out of the cluster of houses and towards a wooded area which in turn led to a river from which Geoff and Godfrey watched the water trickling past and occasionally threw pebbles across its glistening surface. The young boy was fascinated with the way that he could see a mirror-image of himself in the reflection of the shiny liquid, and would stand for some time giggling at himself from the safety of the riverbank. There were few fishermen trying their luck in this particular area and sometimes the pair would walk for half an hour without meeting a single soul. Nevertheless it was peaceful and little Godfrey always returned home with a new word or two to impress his mother and siblings. Olive was delighted that the exercise wore him out and could guarantee that her son would be flat out in his bed soon after returning home and wouldn't wake until seven the next morning. He was always especially tired after their walk along the river.

It was along this very route, right on the edge of the village, that the Walker family lived. The cottage had originally been painted white but now stood looking grey and forlorn with huge flakes of plaster missing from its external walls and ugly rust-coloured stains streaking the places where water over-flow pipes had been allowed to dribble freely down the sides of the building. Paint rolled upwards away from the wooden window sills and dark green moss was growing in abundance on the roof tiles.

Geoff supposed that the dwelling had been a source of pride to its original owner and wondered what fate or circumstance had allowed things to fall in to such a state of disrepair. The garden had been cultivated to create a makeshift allotment but whoever had been responsible for planting the produce had done so in a completely haphazard way. Green beans spread themselves horizontally amongst potatoes, while tomato plants hung limply against a wall where mint leaves threatened to dominate. The result was a very fragrant but jumbled mishmash which resembled an earthy market-stall whose owner had simply tipped is wares out as if he had no care for making it look pleasing to the eye.

As they trundled past the cottage gate one sunny evening, Geoff pointed out a large tabby cat that was sprawled lazily across the doorstep.

"Pussycat", said Geoff slowly, allowing his son to carefully form the word, "That's a pussycat."

Godfrey chuckled and grabbed at the slatted gate, his chubby fists circling the upright parts.

"Pusscat", he mouthed. Geoff patted his son on the head and grinned, "That's it lad, well done."

Just then the shabby wooden door opened and an enormous man appeared, pulling at his braces and scratching his belly simultaneously. He looked as though he had just awakened from a month-long slumber and yawned loudly, displaying a mouth full of rotten teeth as he did so. The man prodded the tabby cat with his toe and suddenly realised that he was being watched. Geoff raised his cap politely.

"Evening", said the hulky man, "Out for a stroll?"

"Yes", replied Geoff, "Just teaching this little one about the countryside."

The man stepped gently over the feline, who was none too happy at being disturbed and hissed at him, and strode over to the gate.

"Don't suppose you could use some vegetables?" he asked in a very gruff but placid manner.

"Well, yes actually", grinned Geoff, "I've got a young family."

"Frank", growled the man, offering a very large and calloused hand, "Frank Walker."

Geoff introduced himself, noting that the man had a bit of a musty smell about him and that his clothes were very worn and faded. He wore tartan slippers on his feet, and one had a very noticeable hole in the toe but apart from his tatty appearance, his face was full of laughter and joy and Geoff instinctively knew that this was a person who was as straight as they came.

And so, from that evening, a friendship of sorts was struck up and every fourth night or so, when Geoff happened to walk with his young boy in that particular direction, Frank Walker would join them as far as the river and then present Geoff with a basket of fresh produce on their return to the cottage gate. The conversation was always very general, with neither having much in common with the other, but each gent seemed content to discuss the weather, the state of the country after the war or the result of a local football match. All in all, it was no more than a brief companionship for Geoff, as he secretly found Frank brash and uneducated but Frank was delighted to have a new friend to pass the time of day with, and watching little Godfrey toddle along the riverbank amused him no end, seeing as he had no children of his own.

Slowly, Geoff came to learn of the situation in which Frank lived and couldn't help but feel a pang of sympathy for the gentle giant. You see, when Frank was only nineteen years old his father had passed away from liver disease, leaving his eldest son George to take care of his younger sibling. Mrs. Walker had long since gone, Frank recounted, but Geoff didn't like to ask whether he meant deceased or just left. It seemed that George Walker was a little too fond of his drink according to Frank, and had therefore neglected his duties to both his brother and their home.

Still, Frank seemed happy enough, judging by the sheer size of him he certainly had plenty to eat, and he all but glowed with pride when he talked about his vegetable garden. Of course, Geoff and Olive were very grateful for the juicy tomatoes and crunchy beans that were provided for them free of charge, and in return Olive would send homemade fruit cake, apple pies or pots of jam for Geoff to exchange with his friend on those evening walks. This unspoken agreement worked very well and both parties looked forward to seeing what the other would have to swap every few days. Even Godfrey enjoyed his time with Frank Walker, especially when the giant man lifted him up to ride on his massive shoulders, while his father chuckled uncontrollably at his side.

The Walker's didn't go to church on Sundays, instead preferring to follow their own pursuits. George could be found drowning his sorrows at the tavern in the next village, flat cap in his head and wellington boots on his feet, while Frank stayed at home to tend his vegetable patch. Sometimes, if the weather was fine, Frank would amble down the hill and stand at the farm gate either watching the cows being milked or looking at the marvellous tactics used by the collie dogs to round up the sheep. He would wave at Geoff or Olive from the farm gate if he happened to see them in the garden or garage, but Frank would never step one single foot up the cul-de-sac.

Olive had obviously become inquisitive about the Walker brothers, especially as her husband and son were regularly taking walks with one of them, and over a coffee with Mrs. Hamilton one morning she used the opportunity to ask about their life. Mrs. Hamilton had lived in the village all of her fifty years, and knew everybody who resided there. She wasn't a woman to relish gossip and knew that Olive was the same, therefore knew that whatever she chose to tell her would not be spread around. She also knew that Olive had been disturbed by some of the villagers' secrets but had kept her own opinions under wraps, after all what the eye didn't see...

"Old Henry Walker was a rum old thing", she began, "Out all hours drinking and causing havoc. He could talk the hind leg off a donkey when he'd had a beer or two, my Arthur used to make sure he'd left the pub an hour before Henry, just so he didn't have to listen to him cursing all the way up the lane."

Olive smiled, trying to imagine a man who resembled his sons, wobbling as he tried to stagger home.

"Now Betty, his wife, was a tiny little woman, very pretty in her own way", Mrs. Hamilton continued, "Always fussing over the boys and rushing around keeping their home in order. I liked her, she was pleasant to talk to and never had a bad word to say about anyone."

"What happened to her?" Olive heard herself ask, "She... she didn't die, did she?"

"No dear, she ran off to Canada with Elsie Corbett's son many years ago. She couldn't take the boys, as she knew Henry would have tracked her down and goodness only knows what would have happened."

Olive gasped. She could just imagine the look on Elsie Corbett's face when she'd found out.

"Anyway, Henry started to drink even more", Mrs. Hamilton explained, "It was the whisky that sent him to an early grave. That house just went to pot without Betty, it's an absolute disgrace inside."

Olive tried not to think about the heartache of a woman having to walk away from her children. It seemed too terrible to contemplate. She knew that if ever she found herself in a situation where Geoff had got himself another woman, she would fight to the death to have her beloved Eileen, Barbara and Godfrey with her. Maybe the things that Betty went through in her marriage were unbearable, Olive mused, something must have pushed her to make such a drastic decision. She returned home deep in thought.

One evening, as Geoff and Godfrey approached the hedgerow that bordered the Walker's cottage, a different figure could be seen standing at the gate. This man was a great deal slimmer than Frank but he bore the same rugged features and had identical watery grey eyes. It was George.

At first, Geoff was unsure whether to stop and hand over the three jars of pickles that his wife had carefully labelled and topped with a circle of gingham cloth. After all, he had never met George Walker and Frank had given the impression that his brother was an unsociable sot at times. However, as they drew closer, George lifted a little basket up from his side and beckoned Geoff to take it.

"Our Frank's with Matilda tonight", the man growled, "Said I should give you this to take home."

"Oh, right," replied Geoff relaxing slightly, "Olive made you some piccalilli and chutney."

George Walker didn't smile, in fact he didn't speak again either, but simply concluded the transaction by snatching the jars and pushing the basket into Geoff's arms. With that, he shuffled back inside the cottage and slammed the door. Geoff was left standing at the gate, holding his son's chubby hand on one side and an armful of vegetables on the other. He felt very confused, but not about George. You see, Frank had never mentioned having a young lady to go courting with but it seemed that this was exactly the scenario. Well, well, thought Geoff to himself as he tugged Godfrey towards home, I wonder what kind of woman he found.

As was his habit, Geoff walked different routes with his son for the next few nights and didn't pass by the Walker's cottage until later that week. Olive had been baking in the afternoon and now Geoff carried a cherry cake wrapped in brown paper as he set off up the hill.

Frank was already waiting at the gate, his bulky frame plainly visible from the narrow lane and, as Geoff drew near, Godfrey started toddling faster to where the large man stood with outstretched arms.

"Evening", grinned Frank cheerfully, "Sorry I missed you the other night, Matilda wasn't well so I decided to sit with her until she felt better. She can be a right miserable thing when she's under the weather."

"No problem", said Geoff, not wanting to pry but feeling a little curious all the same, "I hope she's on the mend. There's been a nasty flu bug going around'.

"Oh aye, right as rain now", chuckled Frank, as he unlatched the gate to join father and son on the lane, "She's a tough old girl. You wouldn't know she'd been ill if you saw her now."

Geoff smiled politely but couldn't help feel a bit surprised at the way in which Frank had referred to his lady friend. Still, given that the Walkers were what Olive would term 'rough around the edges' or 'common as muck' he wouldn't be at all shocked if Matilda were a simple farm girl who had been brought up with the same outlook on life and moral values as her suitor.

Geoff did the honours of passing over the cake and in return received a cardboard box containing several enormous leeks and a dozen large duck eggs. It really was great that Frank always managed to give them something different at every meeting, Geoff mused gratefully, Olive had hardly needed to buy much at all from the market since he'd become acquainted with Frank Walker, it really was a blessing. He was certain that Frank and his brother enjoyed Olive's wonderful home bakes too, as Frank was always sure to send his compliments to her and asked with fervour what she might be baking next.

As they walked along the riverbank that evening, stopping every now and then to let Godfrey pick a flower or chase a butterfly, Geoff felt that something had changed between himself and Frank. It was almost as if the big hulk at his side had now let his guard down and walked in a more relaxed fashion. Geoff could only surmise that it was due to his friend's revelation about having a girlfriend and it wasn't long before his suspicions were confirmed.

"Have you been married long Geoff?" Frank asked timidly as they stepped on to the rickety wooden bridge to throw sticks over the side, "You seem very happy with your missus."

"Ten years next month", answered Geoff proudly, "And I still love her to bits. My best friend too."

"Ten years", repeated Frank as he mulled it over, "That's a long time."

"Oh it soon goes", replied Geoff, kicking at a piece of dried mud with his toecap. "Especially when you've got little ones. You have to work at it mind, don't ever take anything for granted."

Frank nodded and then seemed to suddenly be deep in thought, as he turned around on the bridge to watch his stick go bobbing down the river.

"Do you think you might start a family?" ventured Geoff, "You know with Matilda?."

The other man looked dumbfounded, just for a few seconds, and then a wide grin appeared on his dim-witted face. Geoff smiled back, hoping that he hadn't touched on a nerve, but all that did was start Frank off in a fit of laughter. Geoff chuckled too, but only because his friend had now bent over for such a belly laugh that the seam of his trousers had split from top to bottom, exposing a glimpse of enormous off-white underpants. As for Frank, well, he just laughed louder and deeper until tears rolled down his fat rosy cheeks. At last, after quite a while of hooting and gasping, both men came to their senses again and turned their attention to a very bewildered Godfrey who stood staring at them with his mouth open wide and a bunch of dandelions in his hand.

"Let's get you home", said Geoff, gently lifting his son up on to his shoulders, "It's getting cold."

As they left the riverbank and walked on to the lane Geoff noticed that, despite Frank walking with one hand covering his exposed behind, the younger man had a spring in his step and was whistling a tune. Perhaps it had been the talk of family that had put his friend in such good spirits, Geoff pondered. He would have to try to remember to ask Olive if she knew Matilda,

At the cottage gate, Frank stooped to pick up the basket that Geoff had left behind a bush while they had taken their stroll, and then paused to pat his friend on the arm.

'I've had a right laugh tonight", he bellowed far too loudly, given their close proximity to each other.

Geoff nodded but said nothing, he was still in the dark as far as the cause of Frank's high spirits were concerned. He then let out a sigh and shook Frank Walker's hand.

"See you Thursday then," smiled Frank, slowly counting off the days on his enormous fingers.

"Aye you certainly will, weather allowing. Goodnight lad, and look after that young lady of yours", Geoff called as he turned to start his descent down the hill.

At the mention of Matilda, Frank burst out in a fit of hysterics again and couldn't even get his words out clearly to bid Geoff and Godfrey farewell.

"Right…Matilda…family…ha, ha", he gasped, closing the latch on the gate with one hand while clutching his side with the other, "Night…ha, ha, oohh Geoff."

Geoff watched his friend chuckle all the way to the door of the cottage and then turned away slowly and shook his head. One of these days Frank would be sure to explain the source of his amusement but for now it was just a pleasure to see the young man enjoying himself.

Later that evening, as Olive sat mending socks in the kitchen, Geoff helped himself to a bottle of stout from the pantry and sat down at the table by her side, the earlier conversation with Frank still very fresh in his mind. Olive too had been brooding over what Mrs. Hamilton had told her.

"Have you ever seen Frank Walker with a young lady?" he asked curiously.

Olive looked up from her darning and shook her head, brown curls dancing softly around her ears.

"Don't be daft, love", she giggled, "What kind of girl would be seen out with a good-for-nothing lump of lard like that? He's got no chance of meeting anyone unless he smartens himself up."

Geoff snorted, that was so true, but still he felt quite sorry for Frank.

"I don't suppose he's much to look at, or got anything in the way of prospects", he pondered, "But he's got a heart of gold and a great way with the youngsters. Our Godfrey thinks the world of him."

"That may be so", laughed Olive, "But I still can't see anyone in a hurry to get him up the altar."

"He's got a girl though", confessed her husband suddenly, feeling slightly guilty at betraying Frank's confidence, "Some lass called Matilda."

"Well I never!" gasped Olive, setting down the bundle of socks that she had been working on, "The poor dear must need her head looking at, where's she from? Do you reckon she lives in the village?"

"He didn't get around to telling me that" replied Geoff, "I'm guessing she's local."

The couple looked at each other and burst out laughing, neither saying anything more on the subject but both finding it a great source of amusement.

That night, as they lay side by side in their comfortable bed, with the lights out and both thinking the other had already drifted into slumber, husband and wife thought of nothing but the girl whom Frank Walker might be contemplating marrying. And as they eventually started to dream, Olive imagined trying to find enough reams of fabric to make a dress for a girl twice the size of Frank Walker. At her side, Geoff dreamt about hiring a lorry to take the couple home from church on their wedding day, the wheels and engine screeching under the strain of the combined weight it was expected to haul up the lane to the little white cottage on the hill.

Thursday evening soon came around, but the wind had started to blow cold, and by the time Geoff and Godfrey had reached the Walker's cottage he was almost changing his mind about going to the river.

Frank was waiting at the gate, still in his shirtsleeves and grinning widely. Apparently he was never affected greatly by the cold weather and wore the same clothes all year round.

"It's a bit nippy tonight", began Geoff, "Think I might take our Godfrey back home."

Frank opened the gate and gestured for them to step on to the gravel yard.

"Why don't you come in and have a drink?" he offered, "I can make your little 'un some warm milk."

Geoff didn't quite know how to react, Olive had told him what their neighbour had said about the condition of the Walker's cottage, but he really didn't want to offend Frank by refusing his hospitality.

'Don't trouble yourself on our behalf", he answered, trying to be tactful, "We'll get off home."

"Nonsense", laughed Frank, "Come on, I'll put the kettle on." With that, the large man didn't wait for a response and headed back towards the front door of his home. Geoff followed, wondering what awaited them inside.

As he passed through the hallway, the first thing that hit Geoff's senses was the smell. It was a strange aroma, sort of dirty clothes mingled with tobacco, unpleasant but not quite bad enough to take his breath away. He looked down at his son, who seemed completely unfazed by his surroundings, and guided him towards a large kitchen where Frank was already fussing over preparations for his guests. Geoff looked around. The kitchen was tidy, but looked as though it hadn't had a thorough clean for half a century. Nothing crowded the work surfaces, but the windows hardly let in any light as they were so dirty on the both the inside and outside. There was a huge pan on the stove-top, with huge streaks of brown liquid staining the sides, it looked as though it had been there for some time. Geoff looked down at the bare floorboards underneath his feet. They had been scrubbed bare, but balls of cat fur, dust and cobwebs had gathered in the corners and up against the chair legs. Olive would have a field day in here, he thought, although it would take her a full week to get things spotless.

"Sit down, make yourself at home", Frank insisted, "Push that damned cat off the chair if you need to."

Geoff carefully picked up the grumpy feline and put her on his lap. He had a soft spot for animals and it wasn't long before the cat had curled up and was starting to purr like a tractor. Godfrey clambered on to the chair next to his father and gently stroked the cat under its chin.

Frank laughed, "She's a bad-tempered old thing, but she seems to have taken to you two."

He set two large chipped mugs down in front of Geoff and a smaller cup for the little boy, pouring warm milk in to it from a pan. He then put a milk bottle, a bag of sugar and a pot of tea on the table.

"Ah, this is nice", he smiled, "We don't get many guests up here, unless you count the postman."

The two men chatted for a while about general things. Frank was contemplating whether it was the right time of year to plant cabbages and Geoff told him a bit about a project he was working on at the foundry.

"Do you work Frank?" he asked casually.

The other man nodded, "I help out at Adams's farm in Brayton. Cycle up there every morning at six, then finish about four in the afternoon. I love working with the animals."

Geoff tried to picture Frank Walker on a bicycle, that would be a sight worth seeing, he thought.

"It's a fair old ride out there", he commented, "Must take you an hour or so."

'Ay, it does", Frank agreed, "Sometimes the boss gives me a lift home if he's coming this way."

And so the conversation continued, with Geoff learning about Frank's enthusiasm for his job and Godfrey content to drink his milk and play with the furry animal now stretched out on his father's knees.

"And how's Matilda?" Geoff ventured, genuinely interested in his friend's new relationship.

"She's grand", beamed Frank, "I never loved a female more than I love her. Lovely she is."

Geoff smiled, "Perhaps you could bring her over for a bite to eat one night, Olive would be glad of a bit of company and she's always got a good dinner on the go."

Frank chuckled, "Thanks for the offer. But we don't tend to go out, she's very shy you see."

Geoff bowed his head and decided not to push it any further, it was time he got home anyway.

"Well, see you Sunday all being well", he said moving the cat gently on to the chair cushion as he got up, "I bet Olive will have baked something nice for you as well."

Frank followed the father and son towards the door, "I'm going to get myself off to bed before George gets in from the pub", he declared, "I'll see you at the weekend, should have some eggs for you."

'Grand", replied Geoff, ushering Godfrey towards the gate, "I'll see you then. Goodnight."

It had been an unexpected visit, giving Geoff cause to wonder even more about the Walker's lives and he was still deep in thought when he arrived home. After sharing the evening's events with Olive he wished he hadn't as she chided him for letting their son enter such a dirty environment, wondering what kind of diseases he was exposed to, and the couple ended up not speaking to each other for the rest of the night.

When Sunday night came around Geoff and Godfrey ventured up the hill again towards the Walker's home. Laden with a fresh batch of Olive's scones and a jar of strawberry jam, Geoff was looking forward to seeing if his acquaintance was still in good spirits, and now little Godfrey toddled earnestly towards the heavy wooden gate in search of his giant friend. Usually, by the time Geoff and his young son had reached the cottage, Frank would be there waiting for them with a big grin on his face. Tonight, however, the cottage path bore no burly figure and even the Walker's enormous tabby cat was nowhere to be seen. Geoff waited for a couple of minutes, wondering if he should knock on the door but felt a bit hesitant to do so as that was never the way between the two men. It was generally considered that if Frank was joining them, he would be waiting outside.

Just as he had made a firm decision to leave his parcel on the cottage step and continue on his walk to the river with his son, Geoff heard the door latch click.

Two seconds later, the door opened and the unshaven features of George Walker appeared. He didn't look at all amused to see two visitors standing at the gate and his face reddened.

"I suppose you've come to get the gossip", he slurred, very obviously the worse for too much beer, "Didn't take long did it, before one of you lot came poking your nose around here."

"Sorry", replied Geoff rather indignantly, standing up straight and pushing out his chest, "I haven't got a clue what you're talking about."

"Pull the other one", sniffed George, running his dirty fingers through his mop of greasy hair, "The whole bloody village must have seen our Frank being arrested this afternoon!"

"What?! gasped Geoff, now feeling quite startled, "Why on earth has he been arrested?"

"Mind your own bloody business" roared the other man, shaking his fist, "Now bugger off!"

"No need to take that tone", snapped Geoff as he took Godfrey's hand, 'We're going."

"And don't bother coming back", shouted George, "You're not welcome here, none of you!"

Geoff scooped his son up in to his arms and strutted back towards home. He was too fired up to go walking along the riverbank now and intended to see if any of the neighbours knew what had happened at the Walker's cottage. Olive certainly hadn't mentioned anything as they'd chatted over tea earlier, maybe Stan Hargreaves would be able to enlighten Geoff.

Being in such a determined state of mind, Geoff had soon deposited Godfrey with the boy's mother and went straight back out to speak to his neighbour.

"Not a clue", tutted Stan Hargreaves, shaking his large bald head, "I've not long come home from work and the wife's been at her sister's all day. Arrested you say?"

Geoff nodded furiously, "So George Walker reckons."

"Mmm, always thought him to be a good lad, bit simple but never been in trouble before."

"I feel we should try to find out though", said Geoff cautiously, "I mean maybe the lad has taken the flack for someone else's wrongdoing."

"That's as maybe", replied Stan thoughtfully, "I wonder who we could ask?"

"What about his young lady?" retorted Geoff, suddenly remembering Frank's new love, "Have you ever heard Frank mention Matilda?"

"Erm, well yes of course I have. I was there when she gave birth last winter."

"What?" gasped Geoff, almost needing to take a moment to sit down, "They've got a child?"

"What the hell are you talking about Geoff? asked Stan in a perplexed manner, "What child?."

"You said…" trailed Geoff, trying to gather his thoughts, "So Frank and Matilda are married?"

A look of confusion swept across Stan Hargreaves' face, until it suddenly dawned on him that it was his neighbour who was the one completely in the dark about Frank Walker.

"Matilda's a bloody pig", he said gently, "Of the swine variety."

Geoff fainted out cold, his head bouncing on the soft cushion of his neighbour's padded sofa.

Chapter Ten
Malcolm and Mrs. Taft

As Olive wrangled with the billowing sheets, trying desperately to peg them onto the washing-line before the wind tangled them beyond control, she could feel someone watching. She looked up to the skies, where a dark greyness loomed and rain clouds gathered, and then slowly turned around to face her neighbour's window.

A warm, smiling face met her gaze. It was Malcolm. Despite having lived next door to each other for a few years now, they were still as unacquainted as strangers, although Olive and Geoff had heard many admirers commenting on how the young man had given up everything to care for his elderly grandmother. What a lovely lad, thought Olive, there he was working away in the kitchen, preparing another of his savoury pies no doubt. Although she was yet to taste his culinary delights, the smell of herbs and gravy that wafted across from next-door often set Olive's stomach rumbling.

Olive raised her free hand and waved, risking losing control of the linens in her grasp as she did so. Malcolm beamed and frantically waved back, pastry brush in hand and flour peppering the front of his green cable knit sweater. Olive shifted her focus back to the task at hand, if only she could get these damn sheets out for an hour it might at least half dry them, making her morning's work at the mangle worthwhile. Finally she was done and stooped to pick up the laundry basket at her feet. As she looked up again, Olive realised that she was no longer being observed. Malcolm had moved away from her line of vision, probably attending to his elderly grandmother, Mrs. Taft. Oh well, she mused, no rest for the wicked, there were the children's school sweater's to darn, dinner to prepare and Godfrey to attend to. Olive hummed a light tune as she made her way back up the garden path, unaware that another pair of eyes were staring down at her from an upstairs window.

As Olive returned to the warmth of her kitchen to make a brew, her thoughts once again turned to the young man and old lady residing next door. What perfect neighbours they were, she hardly heard a peep from them, not even a murmur of complaint when Olive's youngest daughter Barbara caused havoc, with the short temper of a fiery red-head. Mind you, she saw very little of Mrs. Taft these days unless Malcolm carried her out in to the garden for a few hours of sunshine. He was a good lad. Being the only immediate neighbours with whom they shared a partition wall, Olive and Geoff would have expected more day to day interaction with them, not as intimate as popping in to each other's homes for coffee, but at least to pass the time of day in conversation over the adjoining hedge. Mind you, Olive mused, what she would actually have in common to chat about with either of them somewhat confounded her.

Olive was unsure how Malcolm had come to live with his grandmother, although she wondered whether his simple mind and slow ways had been a source of embarrassment for his parents. In fact, she pondered, perhaps Malcolm's father had been a casualty of the war like so many other young men a decade before, that would perhaps go some way to explaining the absence of parental guidance. Olive and her family had by now been residing in the village for five whole summers and in that time had come to know little of their immediate neighbour's circumstances. It was a different matter with others nearby however, who would spend hours leaning over their garden gates whiling away he time in idle gossip. Olive, after all the strange occurrences that she had endured over the years, didn't like to engage in fruitless chatter. She was partly too busy raising her three young children but mostly afraid of what new sordid secret would surface if she did. Still, she couldn't help but wonder about Malcolm, he couldn't be any more than twenty-five years old, a great bear of a lad with giant hands that ceaselessly toiled, whether it be tending to the flower beds or baking something delicious to satisfy the cravings of Mrs. Taft's savoury tooth. Oh yes, mused Olive, raising the china teacup to her lips, she vaguely remembered Mr. Taft, the young man's grandfather.

Now that was a funny thing. When Olive's family had moved to the cul-de-sac, old Mr. Taft had definitely been living there, she remembered his bird-like features and the green Austin van that he drove to work each day, although she couldn't remember for the life of her what it was that the old man had done to make a living. Over each summer they had spotted him pottering about in his old brown overcoat, and then during the winters he would disappear completely, almost as though he'd been afraid to go out in the cold or decided to hibernate. About three months ago, Olive had heard a commotion next door but, due to the rapidity of its conclusion, hadn't thought it necessary to investigate the cause of the disturbance. She had heard raised voices and something being thrown, but by the time she had raised her husband from his slumber, the walls were silent again and Geoffrey had told her to turn over and go back to sleep.

The next morning just before dawn, as Olive opened the living room curtains, she heard more loud noises and peered around the lace netting to see what was happening. It was hard to see the owner of the voice that bellowed loudest, but she presumed it was Mr. Taft. She suddenly caught sight of him on the driveway, dragging a huge suitcase into the car but then Malcolm appeared and caught his grandfather by the arm, dragging him back towards the house with brute force. There had been a short argument between the two men and then silence. Olive presumed that whatever had caused them to fight was now either forgiven or forgotten. The rest of that day and the few days following she didn't hear a sound from the people residing next door and put the incident to the back of her mind.

It wasn't until Geoff commented on something a week later that Olive was reminded of what she'd seen.

"Old Mr. Taft must have left", he muttered, "Haven't seen his car parked outside for a few days."

Olive told him about the scene she'd seen outside their neighbour's house and then thought hard. She was sure that she had heard the car engine revving up the evening after the argument as she had been running a bath for the girls. She hadn't bothered to look outside.

"So he must have gone the night after that row", she concluded, "What a carry on."

"Perhaps he's found himself another woman", Geoff countered, "That's usually the root of all trouble."

Olive disagreed. "I really don't think he's the type to run off with someone. Besides, I've never seen him raise his voice to Malcolm before."

"Well, whatever it was, it's none of our business, love", Geoff said, "Best keep out of it."

Olive was more than happy not to get involved, she knew enough village secrets to last her a lifetime!

There were rumours of course. People in the village speculated wildly about Mr. Taft's infidelity and the comfort that he found in a bottle of brandy every night. As far as they were concerned, Mr. Taft's departure was nothing unexpected, but Olive couldn't help wonder what had really happened to make him pack up and leave so suddenly. You see, apart from the incident on that early morning, there had been no grand exit, no slamming of doors, no shouting, nothing. The only change had been in the old lady. Mrs. Taft had taken to her bed after the night of the argument, and refused implicitly to get up again. Poor Malcolm had become sole breadwinner, housekeeper and carer overnight, although it was a wonder the pair managed to survive on the money from odd jobs that the youngster brought in. Nevertheless, people were kind, they always found tasks for the willing half-wit and when money was tight, which was often in post-war Britain, they would pay Malcolm in produce from their gardens. And you know, despite his lack of intelligence, Malcolm Taft could turn his hand to anything.

It was over pleasant exchanges at the village shop that Olive encountered the most gossip about the Taft family. Everyone had their own theory and since Mr. Taft's car had disappeared from the driveway, several people reported sightings of it being driven all over the county. One chap even confessed to having seen it while on holiday in Scotland, but the women of the village just raised their eyebrows at him and ensured that he must have been mistaken. Others were certain the motor had been parked outside the house of a young widow in town, but nobody really knew the truth.

Olive thought that she might very discreetly ask Mrs. Hamilton if she knew the situation next door, after all she lived two doors away from them and had been resident there for longer than the other occupants.

"I did hear a bit of a commotion", confirmed the neighbour, folding her arms across her chest, "But I didn't take much notice really, as we all have our ups and downs don't we Olive."

"I just wondered if everything was alright there now", she ventured, "I haven't seen Mr. Taft."

"No, I've not seen him either", said Mrs. Hamilton puckering her lips, "Mind you, he was mucking about with a milk maid from Little Stanton a while back, maybe he's run off with her."

Olive wasn't convinced. If that was the case, why hadn't Mr. Taft just left on the night of the argument, instead of leaving it until the next day. She shared her thoughts with her friend.

"Perhaps he just wanted things to calm down a bit dear", Mrs. Hamilton mused, "You know how men can be, never make up their minds until the last minute."

"Has he ever left before?" asked Olive, running a few different scenarios through her very inquisitive mind, "Or was this the first time anything like this has happened?"

"Well, they've certainly argued before", continued the neighbour, "But as for leaving, no, they'd been married nearly forty years. Fancy him taking flight now then eh?"

Olive left Mrs. Hamilton at her cottage door and trotted back home where she had a list of chores to finish. As she set up the ironing board and pulled the basket of laundry to her side, Olive tried to recount the strange events at the Taft's house in chronological order. So, it had been a Sunday evening that the argument had happened, all three voices of grandmother, grandfather and grandson had been clearly heard through the walls. The next morning she remembered seeing Malcolm frog march his grandad back in to the house as he had tried to leave with a suitcase. Olive racked her brains, trying to recall whose voices she had heard after that but couldn't remember. She'd been busy getting breakfast and sending the girls off to school, and hadn't taken too much notice of events after that. Besides, she was pretty sure that the house next door had been silent for the rest of that day.

But of course, then there was the evening, and the faint sound of a motor car being driven away, but Olive couldn't swear on that to be certain, as she'd had the tap running and was in and out of the bathroom sorting out fresh towels and nightdresses for her daughters. Surely she would have heard if there had been another argument, she pondered, and she was convinced that all had been silent.

Olive was suddenly roused from her thoughts by Godfrey banging some saucepans together on the kitchen floor. Must be time for his afternoon nap if he's getting bored, realised the young mum. As she ascended the staircase leading up to her young son's tiny bedroom, Olive could hear the faint murmur of Mrs. Taft chatting with her grandson in the house next door. I really must pop round and see her, thought Olive, perhaps a bit of female company would rouse her from her bedchamber. But then again, it wouldn't be today, there were far too many tasks to attend to before the girls returned from school.

Later that day, as Olive laid the table with bread and jam for her daughters, she was interrupted by a faint tapping at the back door. Not quite sure whether it was the rap of a visitor or simply a bird on the guttering, Olive took her time in answering and by the time she had put down the tea towel and wiped her hands on her cotton apron, there was no-one there. However, as she was just about to fasten the latch again, Olive glanced down and saw that someone had left a pie on the doorstep. She smiled, this was the first time that her neighbour had shared one of his culinary delights. It was a meat and potato pie, carefully wrapped in gingham cloth, with a thin red ribbon tied to hold the folds together at the top. Olive sighed, Malcolm was such a kind boy, but she dared not tell him that the pie might not be as gratefully received by her family as would usually be expected.

Olive's daughters wouldn't touch the pie. Eileen, the eldest, had recently decided that she was going to save every animal on the planet and wouldn't touch the meat inside. Barbara, however, would eat anything you put in front of her, except pastry. Godfrey had a delicate stomach and was prone to constipation if his mother fed him anything too heavy, and Olive herself was desperately trying to keep her svelte figure intact. No matter how tempting the pie looked, and smelled, she just couldn't risk it, family genetics dictated that one slice would result in an inch of excess fat around her waist. No, Olive had to resist. Nevertheless, she wasn't one to waste good food, so the meat and potato pie would stay wrapped and Geoff could take it to the foundry with him to share with his workmates the next day. And if Geoff just happened to presume that this delicious pie had been baked by his wife's loving hands, who was she to let him think any differently?

Another summer turned to autumn in the village and life went on as usual for Olive and her brood. She never did get around to visiting old Mrs. Taft, it just didn't seem right to go knocking on her neighbour's door after all this time. Besides, Malcolm was always pottering around, he would surely say if something was amiss. Olive still received a savoury pie every now and again, and always sent it with Geoff to share with his grateful colleagues. In fact, Olive was gaining herself something of a reputation as an excellent cook thanks to Malcolm's pies.

One day at the end of October, as she collected eggs from her fluffy-footed bantam chickens, Olive just happened to notice that Malcolm was watching her again. This time he didn't wave but turned rapidly away and then disappeared from view completely. She thought nothing of it, after all the lad wasn't quite the full shilling, until a few minutes later when she felt the all too familiar feeling of someone watching again. This time Olive gathered up her basket, squeezed through the hole in the hedge and marched around the side of her neighbour's house to where Malcolm stood peering at her from behind the chintz curtains in his grandmother's kitchen. She knocked three times and waited. After just a few seconds Malcolm opened the door and peered out.

"Is everything alright, love?" Olive inquired.

"It's my gran", stammered the young man, "She's not well."

"Oh dear, let me in then and I'll take a look at her."

As Malcolm stepped aside, Olive could smell something sickly coming from the rooms beyond. It took her breath away for a moment, but she couldn't for the life of her imagine what could create such a strange and putrid odour. She had certainly never come across a smell like it before. Turning her thoughts away from the stench, Olive followed Malcolm along the hallway and up the stairs to a brown door half way along the landing. She couldn't help noticing the threadbare carpet and flaking paint, but besides the lack of fancy décor, the house itself was spotlessly clean. What a good lad Malcolm is, Olive thought to herself for the umpteenth time, he does look after his poor old gran.

As they neared the door, Olive could hear someone coughing beyond. It was a deep throaty rasping. Mrs. Taft was obviously a very poorly woman.

Malcolm slowly turned the door handle and ushered Olive inside. The room was dark, with just a glimpse of autumn sunlight shining through the faded pink curtains, and as Olive adjusted her eyes to the dim surroundings, a small croaky voice greeted her.

"Hello Mrs. G, I'm so sorry if our Malcolm has dragged you around here unduly."

Olive turned to look at the owner of the voice and momentarily took an intake of breath as she looked towards the bed. Mrs. Taft had become a woman of huge proportions, her great flabby arms pulling restlessly at the tatty purple eiderdown as she struggled to pull herself upright on the mattress.

"It's no trouble", Olive managed to reply, "What ails you, Mrs. Taft?"

"Oh nothing but a bit of indigestion or gastric flu", the old lady gasped, "A bit of milk of magnesia and I'll be as right as rain."

Olive turned to face the young man standing at her side, "Do you know what that is, Malcolm?"

He shook his head in the negative, "No, I've never heard of that."

"Don't worry, I've got some in the cupboard", offered Olive, "I'll fetch it for you."

As she talked, Olive looked around the room, it was scrupulously tidy, apart from a plate with the remnants of an unfinished meat and potato pie lying on the bedside table. She smiled to herself, did these people survive on pies alone? Dear me, what a strange thought. Olive made an effort at polite conversation for a few minutes and then plumped up the pillows at the old lady's back before making a hasty retreat back down the stairs. That same fetid odour had taken her breath away in the bedroom, what on earth could it be?

Olive let herself out through the shabby back door and made her way back towards the hedge, firstly wanting to retrieve her egg basket before going inside her own home to find the medicine that Mrs. Taft needed. She had just reached inside the bathroom cabinet for a bottle of the white liquid when the sound of Godfrey waking from his nap reached her ears. He was such a good child, and never cried for attention but instead could be heard giggling and muttering in his cot as he played with his stuffed monkey. Olive abandoned her task for the moment and went to see if her son was ready to get dressed and go downstairs.

By the time Olive had managed to convince her son to sit on his plastic yellow potty, and then wrestled him in to his dungarees, half an hour had already passed.

"Goodness", exclaimed Olive out loud, glancing at the kitchen clock, "I'd forgotten all about the milk of magnesia."

Racing upstairs to collect the brown bottle, and then back down again to scoop Godfrey up into her arms, Olive was quite breathless by the time she knocked on the Taft's back door for the second time that day. Malcolm must have been waiting patiently for his neighbour to return as he turned the door handle within seconds. Olive thrust the medicine at him and hastily explained how much he should give his grandmother and at what regular intervals throughout the day.

"I'll call round again tomorrow", she promised Malcolm as he grinned at her shyly.

"Thank you, Mrs. G", said Malcolm slowly, "She wouldn't let me fetch the doctor."

"We'll see how she is in the morning lad, I'm sure that will do the trick."

As she turned towards home again, Olive couldn't help but wonder if Mrs. Taft's medical problems hadn't been self-induced, partly from her refusal to get out of bed and partly from her obvious obsession with meat and potato pies. She had never seen a person looking so bloated as the old woman, and her lack of personal hygiene had emanated from the bedclothes every time she shifted her large frame on the mattress. As she reached the comfort of her kitchen, Olive thought about the strange smell again. She had never noticed anything untoward permeating the wall that joined the two houses, however the inside her neighbour's home had smelled as bad as an abattoir. Yes, Olive realised, it was not dissimilar to the smell of rotting meat. Perhaps she should coax Malcolm to check the pantry and cold store for signs of rancid foodstuffs, there might be some kind of chops or ham lying long forgotten on a back shelf. Although, how a person living day to day with such a stench couldn't comprehend that they needed to find the source of the smell was beyond her comprehension. Still, she concluded, Malcolm was naive and with his grandmother resigned to her bed it can't have been an easy life.

When Geoff arrived home, Olive gave him an account of her day and asked if he'd ever noticed any odd aromas coming from next door.

"Not that I've noticed", said Geoff scratching his chin, "But I have seen Malcolm in the back shed chopping up meat, perhaps they're buying it in bulk and not managing to eat it before it goes off."

"Ah, that must be it", nodded Olive, grateful that her husband had at least offered a plausible explanation, "You never mentioned it before though love."

"Why would I?" her husband responded, "Not my business if folk are a bit slack in the way they keep their meat. Might be an idea to check our own stuff as well, love, there have been a couple of lads off with dicky stomachs this week. Not saying it's anything to do with your pie Olive, but I've had the runs a few times myself lately at lunchtimes."

Olive could imagine the workers queueing up to use the single outdoor privy at the foundry, and put her hand up to her mouth to hide her amusement. Then suddenly it dawned on her, of course, she hadn't made the pie had she? It could well be that the Taft's lack of knowledge in keeping and preserving meat had caused those upset belly's at her husband's work. However, she was hardly going to admit that she hadn't made those exquisite pies now was she? Whatever would Geoff think of her?

Olive kept her promise to her neighbour and over the following days, she tried her best to spend half an hour each day visiting poor Mrs. Taft. Most of her time was spent instructing Malcolm to change the old lady's bedsheets, make up a bowl of soapy water so that his grandmother could wash herself or to cook her some hasty pudding, Olive's remedy for all known ailments. Malcolm listened carefully to Olive's directions and did as he was told without a murmur of complaint.

Mrs. Taft, on the other hand, did nothing but moan about these administrations. She didn't want to get out of bed to have the sheets changed, the water for washing was either too hot or too cold, and the hasty pudding either lacked or needed sugar. Olive had to bite her tongue on several occasions.

"Listen dear, we're trying to help you", she reasoned, "You'll feel much better if you're clean and comfortable, now let us take these sheets off your bed, we'll be quick about it."

Mrs. Taft grumbled her reply, "I'm alright as I am, you can change them tomorrow",

Olive huffed and winked at Malcolm, who knew that was a signal to get the sheets off the bed the minute his grandmother got up to go to the pot under the bed. Between them, they quickly learned to have fresh linen on the mattress in three minutes flat before she could raise her voice at them.

As the days passed, Olive became more and more concerned about the old lady's eating habits. She was losing weight and had to climb out of bed to sit on the chamber pot several times a day, but still she was forcing herself to eat Malcolm's meat pies at every mealtime. Olive just couldn't work out what was going on. Malcolm ate the pies too, either covered in homemade pickle or with thick onion gravy, but he seemed to be perfectly alright. Is it the pies? she wondered, perhaps Malcolm just has a stronger constitution than Mrs. Taft. Using her usual sleuthing skills, Olive decided to probe Malcolm about the meat.

"Do you go to the local butcher, dear?" she asked casually one lunchtime as Malcolm climbed the stairs with yet another tray of pie for his aged relative.

"Erm, no", the lad stuttered, "Erm, granny got the meat last month, I'm not sure where from."

"Oh," countered Olive, suddenly having a revelation, "Perhaps it's a bit too old by now Malcolm."

"No, it's alright", the young man said defensively, "I've preserved it in a barrel of salt like she told me."

Olive's stomach tied itself in a knot. She had a horrible vision of raw meat stuffed in to a wooden keg in the old woman's shed. Surely it wouldn't be safe to use after a month, she pondered. She would have to check with Geoff to see what he knew about maintaining the freshness of meat.

"Well, I know you can do that with fish", Geoff muttered in between bites of his pork chop and potatoes that evening, "But I don't think you can keep meat in the same way, not in a barrel anyhow."

Olive pushed her untouched dinner away from her, she'd suddenly lost her appetite.

"You not going to eat that, love?" Geoff grinned, already stabbing the juicy chop with his fork.

The following morning, after dropping Godfrey off at his first session of playgroup at the village hall, Olive reluctantly negotiated her way up her neighbour's path. She was in a tearful frame of mind that day, as instead of crying and clinging to his mother as expected, her precious Godfrey had simply toddled off to climb in to the sand pit without even waving goodbye. The kind middle-aged teacher had assured Olive that this was a good sign, and told her that after all it was only for a couple of hours, but Olive couldn't help feel a tug at her heartstrings as her tiny boy took his first steps to independence. Emotions were running high as she tapped gently on the Taft's back door.

It wasn't long before Malcolm could be heard lumbering down the hallway, and the way in which he beamed at Olive made up for at least a part of the upset that her morning had brought already. He was dressed in brown work trousers, a white shirt with a green woollen cardigan over the top and a pair of tartan slippers. He looked like a man three times his age. Olive wondered if he'd been up all night tending to the old woman's needs.

"Just come to check on your gran", she smiled, "Is she better today?"

"A bit", nodded Malcolm, "I'm not really sure, she's been on the chamber pot for most of the night."

Olive flushed. What condition was she going to find the old lady in this time, she wondered.

"I'd better come and see her then", she responded, stepping over the threshold without waiting to be invited, "We might need to call the doctor out."

Malcolm plodded up the stairs behind Olive and called out to his gran to warn her of the visitor's arrival.

On entering the bedroom, Olive was met with an even more unbearable stench than the previous day and involuntarily gagged as she controlled to keep the bile from rising in her throat.

"Good Lord", she muttered, between breaths, "Let's get some windows open."

Malcolm didn't appear to be affected by the dreadful combination of faeces, rotting meat and sweat penetrating the room, and moved casually over to let in some air as instructed.

"We need to get you some help", gasped Olive, turning to face the sickly old woman, who was now struggling to sit up properly, "There is something seriously wrong."

"I don't want any doctor coming poking around here," she croaked, lifting her head from the pillow.

"Let me help you to sit up", murmured Olive, finding it hard to breath let alone speak to the woman.

Mrs. Taft looked a strange shade of green and held one hand to her chest as she tried to lever herself up into a more comfortable position so that she could respond to Olive.

"Don't try to speak", choked the younger woman, "I'm going to go and fetch someone."

Mrs. Taft simply shook her flabby head and waved her hand at Malcolm to get his full attention.

"Stop", she gabbled, "I'll be alright by tomorrow."

Malcolm moved quickly across the doorway and blocked Olive's escape route.

"Now look here", Olive cried indignantly, "I need to get your granny some help."

"But we don't want anyone around here asking questions", Mrs. Taft puffed, "Not now."

"Heavens above", tutted Olive, "Anyone can see you need to go to hospital, I think you've got food poisoning from those pies you keep eating."

Malcolm and Mrs. Taft exchanged a startled look with each other which Olive noticed straight away.

"What is it?" she demanded, "Did you get the meat off the back of a lorry or something?"

Mrs. Taft was unable to answer, as her bowels loosened under the covers and another foul stench began to permeate the air. Malcolm rushed to her side, grabbing the chamber pot as he went.

Olive didn't hang around to endure any more. She tore down the stairs as fast as her legs would carry her and stood at the Taft's back door taking gulps of air as the wind blew in gusts across her face. After a full minute of simultaneously taking deep breaths and rubbing her stomach, Olive ventured back home. However, she had only just taken off her lightweight raincoat when the urge to vomit overcame her and she found herself hurtling upstairs towards the bathroom to release her breakfast into the lavatory.

Feeling slightly better for having an empty stomach, Olive washed out her mouth with water from the tap and wandered in to her and Geoff's bedroom to find a clean cotton handkerchief with which to wipe the tears from her eyes, before having to stroll down to the village shop to use the telephone to call a doctor.

As she lifted a square of lace from the top drawer, Olive became aware of a heated argument coming from the bedroom next door. It was clear that Malcolm and his ailing grandmother were exchanging words but she could make out no more than a few syllables at any given time. It was obvious that Mrs. Taft had no difficulty getting her point across now, she had either made a miraculous recovery or was driven by something compelling, perhaps anger or need.

Olive was perplexed. Why would they be quarreling when the old lady was obviously in need of medical attention? There was only one way to find out. Olive padded to the bathroom to retrieve a glass from the shelf and brought it back to the adjoining wall where she shamefully pressed it against the flowery purple and gold wallpaper. She had been shown how to this by her brothers when she was younger, it was a great way of finding out what their parents planned to buy them for Christmas or birthdays.

Olive put her ear on the centre of the glass. Her eyes grew wide as she carefully listened.

"You stupid boy", chided the woman's voice, "Now look what you've gone and done, there will be all sorts of questions if that woman brings the doctor here"

"I didn't know what else to do, Gran" whined Malcolm, "You looked terrible lying there in your bed."

"I'll just lay off the pies for a week or two", scoffed Mrs. Taft, "Be as right as rain then."

Olive heard something being picked up and scraped, similar to the sound of cutlery being rattled across the surface of a piece of porcelain.

"Sorry, Gran" the male uttered, "But without the pies, how else are we going to get rid of Grandad?"

Chapter Eleven
The Village Fete

As Geoff entered the kitchen he beamed. Olive was hand-washing a woollen sweater in the kitchen sink, hips swaying to the beat of a jazz tune playing on the radio and wisps of her hair were gently being blown from the breeze coming through an open window. It had literally been months since he'd seen her so relaxed. In fact, only since Geoff had finally agreed that the family would move out of the village had he felt a shift in his beloved wife's mood. It had taken many nights of intense discussion and even more silent dinners for him to realise that the only way to return his brood to normality was to move away from these strange occurrences and even stranger neighbours.

Geoff crept forward on tiptoes and slid his arms around Olive's waist. She leaned back to rest her head on his shoulder and sighed, "Mmm, so what do you want then?"

Geoff chuckled, "You know me too well, don't you dear?"

"So?" enquired Olive, unmoving and waiting patiently for a response.

"How about we have one last day out with the kids before we move?" he asked tentatively, trying to keep the tone of his voice upbeat and cheerful.

"Lovely, where were you thinking?" Olive now swung around to face her husband, their eyes meeting.

"Well… look love, don't shoot me, but how about we go to the village fete this afternoon and say our farewells? There are still plenty of people we get on with and we don't have to stay too long…"

Olive visibly tensed, wondering how she could respond without causing an argument.

Silently counting to ten, she then paused, perhaps it wasn't such a bad idea after all. They could leave this wretched place tomorrow and draw a line under everything that had happened.

'Alright", she sighed, "I'll go and put a clean frock on."

Geoff raised a fist in triumph as Olive left the kitchen and went upstairs. He knew it wouldn't be easy for her, but there were still some good people in the village, folks that had helped them out when they'd first moved there, people like Mrs. Hamilton and Bert Langtree. It will be alright, he thought, I'll stay with her for the whole afternoon and we can say our goodbyes properly. He was secretly going to miss his own small group of friends in the village, but given the very disturbing events that had blemished their years at the cottage, Geoff knew it was time to move on. A fresh start for all of them, especially for his wife.

And so, that afternoon, the family set off down the cul-de-sac, past the farm and along the winding lane until they got to the vicarage, where rows of stalls had been set out upon the beautifully tended lawn and all manner of games were already in progress. It was an unusually warm day with blue skies and only one or two soft white clouds floating in the sky, and the villagers were out in their light summer clothes, chatting and laughing while they perused goods and challenged themselves with the games on offer.

The children were really excited, and wanted to try their luck at the coconut shy and guessing how many pink and yellow sweets were crammed in to a huge glass jar. Geoff pressed a few coins in to both of his daughter's palms and sent them off to have fun. Cynthia Todd had thoughtfully set up a play pen for toddlers and babies, so Geoff carried his son over to the little coloured mat where Godfrey immediately began to push a wooden train around the perimeter, giggling as he did so. Olive could see that other parents were also grateful for Cynthia's initiative, it would mean many more happy faces and no worry that their child was getting bored. With their son settled, the couple could now relax and try to enjoy themselves, they had a few good friends that they needed to catch up with too.

It wasn't long until curious folk were waving at them and beckoning them over for a chat. Geoff could see that the majority of the villagers meant well, but he could also tell that they were eager to find out about Olive's 'mystery illness' that had kept her indoors for the past few months. After the last incident, the one involving the Taft family, Olive had kept to herself, never answering the door when anyone knocked, and always sending one of the girls outside to peg out washing or collect eggs. She had stayed safely inside like a recluse, only taking visits from her immediate family members and leaving Geoff to explain her absence at church and village hall gatherings. Mrs. Hamilton had been given a key, just to put Geoff's mind at rest and once a day, usually at lunchtime, she would let herself in to the cottage and join Olive for a pot of tea. They rarely discussed village life in any detail, as it upset Olive's constitution, but the two women would pass an hour in civilized chatter about the weather, knitting patterns and sometimes exchanging recipes. Olive's deep passion for cooking had waned somewhat over the weeks and although she still produced delicious fayre for her family, her own appetite was meagre and bland. And so, here they were, in the midst of the village fete, mingling with their fellow villagers. It's got to be progress, mused Geoff as he acknowledged folk passing on either side of them, let's hope that Olive feels the same. Deftly bringing greetings to a swift close before Olive could get emotional, Geoff still felt as though he were treading on a minefield. What they needed was to take part in the activities and relax.

Taking his wife by the hand, Geoff led her over to a tombola table where Elsie Corbett was in full swing, still wearing her familiar shopkeeper's apron, spinning a little wooden barrel to jumble up the raffle tickets lodged inside. After a quick and very courteous exchange of greetings, Geoff handed over a couple of coins to try his luck at winning a prize. Elsie flung the barrel swiftly on its hinges and opened up the sliding door, nodding kindly at Olive to pluck out her tickets from inside. Olive gently put her hand inside and pulled out two pink slips of paper.

"Nothing for that one", chirped the little shopkeeper, as Olive revealed the first number, "Ooh, but the second one's a winner."

Olive smiled at Geoff as Elsie Corbett rummaged amongst the various prizes to find the number that matched the couple's ticket. With a loud "Aha!" she deftly picked up a large tin of shortbread biscuits and handed it over. Olive thanked her and looked down. There it was! The tell-tale sellotape was pressed around the lid of the biscuit tin – Elsie had been at it again! Geoff nudged Olive and winked, causing any tension she felt to immediately be released. Olive shrugged and slid the shortbread back on to the tombola table with the other prizes. I won't make a fuss today, she thought, not on the eve of our move away. She turned to look at the shopkeeper. Elsie Corbett was already back in action, rolling the barrel for her next customer, oblivious to Olive and Geoff's sideward glances. Now that they could see the funny side of things, Elsie's strange habits had caused them both to giggle, and they hurried off laughing loudly.

Suddenly a shrill, and very posh, voice bellowed across the lawn, "I say Olive, over here my dear."

Olive cringed, she would know that voice anywhere. "Hello Gertrude, how are you?"

"Oh, I just can't believe you're leaving Olive, I was just saying to Mrs. Higginbotham yesterday, the church brigade will miss your help, and of course Mr. Crawford and I will miss you too."

Olive tried not to recall the terrible vision of the Crawford's and their guests prancing around in the nude, and she looked down at her shoes to avoid eye contact as Jesus Crawford now came strolling over.

Geoff took the initiative and chatted about general topics for a few minutes before making their excuses to leave the eccentric couple. Gertrude Crawford kissed Olive on the cheek and wished her well.

"Goodness", gasped Olive when they were finally out of earshot, "She makes me cringe."

Geoff put his arm around Olive's shoulder, "Mrs. Hamilton's over there, let's go and chat to her."

Relieved to see her friend, Olive greeted Mrs. Hamilton with a wide smile, she was genuinely going to miss her good friend and confidante, and seemingly the only sane person in the village.

"I do hope you'll keep in touch Olive", she gushed, "I've really enjoyed having you as a neighbour, oh, and of course a very good friend. I wish you both all the best for the future."

"Thank you", replied Olive, feeling quite sad, "You've always been there for me, I'll miss you so much."

Geoff coughed, "I'm just going over to see Bert, won't be a minute."

Olive watched him walk away and turned back to her friend, "It's certainly been interesting living here."

Mrs. Hamilton nodded and put her hand on Olive's arm, "Look over there, at the vicar."

Olive craned her neck to a stall in the far corner of the garden where Mrs. Hargreaves stood behind a table selling second-hand books. She was dressed in another one of her figure-hugging dresses with a wide patent belt clinching her waist tightly. Olive could see Reverend Todd standing next to her beaming, but didn't understand why her friend had gestured towards them.

"Look where his right hand is", whispered her neighbour, "On that woman's bottom!"

Sure enough, as she looked below Mrs. Hargreaves' waist, Olive could just see the tips of the vicar's fingers as they rested upon the woman's ample buttocks. She gasped, had they no shame!

"You just get used to folk after a while", commented Mrs. Hamilton, "Doesn't matter where you live my dear, everyone has their strange little ways."

Olive disagreed. This was the only place that she had ever lived where people's personal pursuits had started to affect her. Never before had she felt so mentally challenged, it just wasn't normal.

"Come on, let's get a drink", her friend sighed, "You definitely look like you need one."

Olive found herself being steered towards a small tent where refreshments were being served. It was much cooler inside, and both women were glad to be able to get out of the warm sunshine. Two very familiar faces stood looking at them from behind a display of homemade wines and ginger beer.

"Hello ladies", said Anna Muller, "Would you like to try one of Wolfgang's special liqueurs?"

The tall foreigner looked tired and drawn but still outshone all of the rest of the village women with her poise and elegance. Today she wore a wrap-over dress that showed just the right amount of neckline without being too revealing, the fabric was a deep purple and Olive wondered where Anna Muller went shopping to be able to find such stylish clothing.

"They are especially good this year", she continued, "He has been perfecting the recipes."

Mrs. Hamilton was first to accept, "I'll try the sloe wine, please. Olive, what will you have, dear?"

Olive looked down at Anna Muller's gloved hands, made from intricate white lace, even on a hot day like today the beautiful Russian had still managed to keep her delicate wrists covered, hiding her history.

"I'll have the same", Olive smiled, "And I'll buy a small bottle for us to drink at home."

Anna Muller carefully poured the wine in to two small glasses and offered the ladies a ginger biscuit.

"Go on", she encouraged, "You'll find that the ginger goes very well with the sloe berries."

Both women took a ginger round and alternately nibbled and sipped, as the Russian carefully wrapped Olive's purchase in tissue paper and took the money from her gratefully.

Wolfgang Muller peered at them over his thick round spectacles but said nothing for a while. He stood proud and erect, his backbone as stiff as an iron poker.

"Do you like my wine?" he eventually asked, running his tongue quickly across his lips "I pick the berries from bushes by the river. I think it is important to use the freshest ingredients."

They nodded in unison. "It's very good", replied Mrs. Hamilton finishing off the last drop.

"Lovely", added Olive, trying to imagine this very strange man trying to clamber amongst the bushes to pick berries to take home to brew. "I'll look forward to drinking that bottle at Christmas."

"Do come round if you need another bottle", urged Mr. Muller, "You know where we live."

Olive gestured that she would, but knew in her heart that she would never voluntarily step foot inside the German man's house, or indeed inside any of the other cottages in this strange old village. She looked hard at Wolfgang Muller, trying to see if his inner wickedness actually penetrated his outer layer, but he just looked like a boring middle-aged man with very little personality.

"Thank you", she ventured, smiling once more at Anna Muller as she tucked the bottle into her bag. "It's been very nice knowing you."

The foreign woman hesitated, looking as though she were suddenly going to say something profound and meaningful but instead she just inclined her head and said, "You too."

"There you are", gasped Geoff, rushing in to the tent, "I've been looking all over for you, and here you are supping alcohol in the middle of the day!"

Olive blushed, it really wasn't like her to be drinking wine at all, she thought.

"I'm only pulling your leg", her husband teased, "You having a good time then, love?"

Olive said that she was, and wondered if they should go and check on the children.

"They're fine", chuckled Geoff wiping a bead of perspiration off his brow, "I just been and checked on them dear. Godfreys having a picnic with the other toddlers and the girls are playing on the coconut shy with Billy Langtree. Why don't we get something to eat?"

Olive was feeling rather hungry, and felt that she should eat in order to absorb some of the alcohol.

They made their excuses to Mrs. Hamilton and left her talking to Anna Muller about the merits of wine.

"There's a hog roast over by the fence", suggested Geoff, feeling the saliva gathering in his mouth at the thought of a fresh pork bap covered in apple sauce, "Are you peckish?"

Olive said she was and they headed towards the gigantic pig, gently spit-roasting over hot coals. As they approached, a very scrawny figure bent over a low table slicing bread rolls. Geoff soon recognised the untidy clothes and familiar features of George Walker. He turned to look his potential customer squarely in the eye, puffing his chest out like a pigeon as he did so.

"Ow do", grunted the shabby little man, "Are you wanting a pork bap?"

Geoff glanced at the barbecued meat and shook his head, "Not just at the moment thanks."

"But I thought you..." started Olive.

"Just lost my appetite", Geoff whispered pulling her gently away, "I've realised that might be Matilda."

Olive resisted the urge to retch and instead breathed deeply through her nostrils until the feeling had passed. She looked at Geoff, who was also looked very pale and sickly.

"Do you really think it might be?" she uttered, "How dreadful."

"I guess we'll never know", sighed her husband, "But Frank got ten years inside didn't he?"

"Yes, he did", Olive reminded him, "And we all know it was deserved."

"Don't think I'll ever be able to eat pork again", Geoff retorted, "Come on Olive."

The couple sauntered across the grass to collect their son from Cynthia Todd's care. Godfrey was rolling around the play pen with another little boy and it looked as though they were pretending to be fishes swimming in the sea. Cynthia Todd looked up from the stool where she was seated.

"Oh dear", she tutted, "Is it time for you to go home now Godfrey?"

The infant whizzed around at the sound of his name being spoken and giggled when he realised that his mother and father were watching him. He pulled himself to his feet and toddled towards them, arms outstretched, his chubby toes curling under as he stumbled forward.

"Good lad", enthused Geoff, "Come on then, let's get you home."

Godfrey chuckled as his father picked him up and set the child in the crook of his arm.

"Thank you Mrs. Todd", smiled Olive, "We appreciate you looking after him."

Cynthia Todd stood up and smoothed down her skirt, "No trouble at all", she replied earnestly.

"Goodbye", said Olive, turning to walk away from the clergyman's wife.

"I do hope you'll be happy in your new home", called Mrs. Todd, "Do come back some time."

Olive was just about to respond, after all she had nothing against the vicar's wife personally, but was stopped by the presence of Stan Hargreaves strolling towards her. He raised his cap and beamed from ear to ear. However, it wasn't Olive that he was grinning at, it was Cynthia Todd behind her who now stood twiddling her pearl necklace and blushing profusely.

Olive carried on walking, trying to ignore their little tryst. None of it mattered now, she was leaving.

She followed Geoff down past the tombola stall where the old shopkeeper was still busy trying to convince villagers to buy a raffle ticket, and down a short slope to where Eileen and Barbara sat eating toffee apples on a bale of straw with Billy from the farm.

"Ahh, it's not time to go already, is it?" whined Barbara, "I've still got some pennies to spend."

"And me", chimed Eileen, "Dad can we stay for a while longer?"

Geoff scratched his head, he was soft when it came to keeping his children happy and just seeing them looking so joyful pretty much melted his heart. He wondered how Olive was feeling, she'd been out for a couple of hours and hadn't eaten anything all day.

"I can bring the girls back in an hour if you like", offered Billy, seeing that Olive and Geoff both looked a bit peaky. He didn't like to ask if something was wrong but sensed a slight tension in the air.

"That would be alright, wouldn't it?" Geoff asked, nudging his wife, "We could put our feet up for an hour before we have to finish packing." Olive was quick to agree, and she thanked Billy for his kindness.

Making their way back through the stalls and games, Olive looked around. There were a good many people that she hadn't noticed when they were walking around before, and it surprised her somewhat. The Crawford's were still mingling in the heart of the crowd and Jesus's voice could be heard above the others, chortling at some revelation or another. Although obviously now fully dressed, the thought of his scrawny body prancing around the tennis court did nothing to alter Olive's mindset. How many times had Geoff told her just to let it go? It must be a dozen or more by now, she thought. And she had tried to forget about it, she truly had. But then the foundry Christmas party had come along and changed all that, with Mrs. Higginbotham going on and on about her best friend Gertrude Crawford and virtually forcing Olive to join them for a game of tennis in the spring. Thankfully, nothing more had been mentioned since and Olive had been able to change the time of her trips to collect the flowers from the vicarage without having to encounter the nudist couple. She had made up some tale about her sister visiting on Fridays and the vicar had accepted the alteration to their agreement without challenge.

There were lots of goods still to be discovered too. But Olive didn't feel much up to conversation with Mrs. Hargreaves or any of the other ladies manning their stalls in the sunshine. There were a few friendly faces however, and Olive thought she might like to buy a little something to take home with her. She looked around for a friendly face or someone that was selling something she fancied.

One such person was displaying her needlework on a cork board, in the hope that someone would want to buy an embroidered cover for their armchair, a carefully stitched silk bag or a patchwork quilt. Olive watched for a few seconds. The careful way in which the individual moved was very familiar and brought flashbacks of afternoons chattering about fashion whilst sharing tea and scones. Olive indicated to Geoff that she would catch him up in a minute, first she just wanted to stop and see someone.

"I'll take our Godfrey home if you're alright", called Geoff, raising his eyebrows and swinging around to show his wife that their son was now fast asleep in his arms, "Get a cake or something for tea, will you?"

"Good idea", Olive nodded, "I'll see what I can find."

She turned back towards the embroidery stand and smiled kindly at Marilyn Roberts, who stood quite still, dressed in a pretty blue gingham dress, trimmed with a little hem of lace. Olive looked down at the large masculine hands and slightly hairy wrists, and attempted to be polite.

"Hello", she ventured, "You've got some beautiful things on sale here",

"Olive", gasped the stallholder, "I heard you're leaving the village."

She answered in the affirmative and picked up a quilted tea cosy made from squares of flowered material in various shades of blue. "This is lovely", Olive mused, "how much is it?'

"Nothing", replied Marilyn Roberts, "I want you to have it as a gift."

"Oh, I couldn't possibly..."started Olive, "I mean there really is no need."

"I insist", pushed the other, "You were so very kind to me."

"I'm sorry that I never came back", explained Olive, "It just didn't seem right, I just..."

"I understand", said Marilyn Roberts awkwardly, "It must have been quite a shock."

The two acquaintances stood in silence for a few seconds before Olive made her excuses and walked away. It had been lovely having a friend like Marilyn, she thought, not a very conventional friendship in the end but certainly fun while Olive had been in the dark about her real identity. It hadn't really mattered that Martin Roberts liked to dress as a woman, and give him his due he was convincing, she pondered, but Olive didn't like the idea of having afternoon tea with another man. After all, the only man in her life was Geoff, and for as long as she lived, she intended to keep it that way.

Tucking the tea cosy under her arm, Olive carried on across the lawn, bidding farewell to onlookers as they caught her eye, and then suddenly remembering that she had promised to buy something for the family's tea. She looked around to see where a cake or some biscuits might be purchased. With all of her pots and pans already loaded in to the back of Geoff's car, she certainly wouldn't be cooking anything this evening, maybe she should take something savoury as well. There were still a few stalls that she hadn't yet explored but she felt in a hurry to get home now, Olive didn't feel so confident without her husband at her side, as it had been quite a while since she'd ventured out alone.

A cake stall came in to view, which looked promising as it held lots of varieties of both sponge and fruit cakes. Thinking she could please both her children and husband if she bought from here, Olive headed towards the array of goodies to make her selection. Rita Butterworth glared back at her.

"Oh. Hello Ms. Butterworth", faltered Olive, "I just need to buy some cakes for my family."

The old woman sniffed and thrust her hands deep in to her cardigan pockets, her expression unchanging and bearing no friendliness towards her new customer.

"Well, there are plenty of cakes here", she chirped, "Biscuits too if you fancy them, and don't worry they weren't cooked in my house if that's what you're worried about."

"I wasn't thinking any such thing", Olive lied instinctively, "I'll have a look at what you've got."

Rita Butterworth turned her attention towards Mrs. Langtree who had now sidled up to the cake stall, still wearing her long brown fur coat, despite the almost sweltering heat, leaving Olive to make her choices without a critical eye being cast over her as she did so.

"Are you still interested in coming to clean for us?" enquired the farmer's wife.

Olive's ears pricked up but she pretended to be engrossed in studying a fruity Dundee cake.

"Oh yes dear", chattered Rita Butterworth, "I can start this Monday if you like."

"That's wonderful", grinned Mrs. Langtree, "I am very particular about the standard of cleaning mind."

"You've no need to worry on that score", fussed the old lady, "My own house is spick and span."

"That's settled then. I'll take three iced buns and I'll see you on Monday."

With the transaction and job offer concluded, Mrs. Langtree swished away in her furry outfit.

Olive cringed. Rita Butterworth, a hoarder, going to clean for someone else? Surely she'd been hearing things? The dreadful condition of the schoolmistress's house still gave her cause to flinch sometimes.

She looked up from the cakes and found the old woman glaring at her, ready to defend herself against Olive's harsh words, but none came.

"Have you got something to say?" asked Ms. Butterworth nastily, showing her tiny yellow teeth and the tip of her little pink tongue, "Very quiet now aren't you Miss. Hoity Toity?"

Olive looked around to see if anyone else could hear the schoolmistress's harsh words but no-one seemed to be within earshot. Mrs. Langtree was out of view now and to try to catch up with her would have meant running across the vicarage lawn like an idiot.

Anyway, panicked Olive, to tell her what? That her new cleaning lady was a collector of… of what? Of everything? It just seemed ridiculous, nobody would ever believe her. Rita Butterworth stood very still waiting for the other woman to say something, her hairy little chin trembling with indignity.

Olive rapidly moved away, forgetting all about the cakes until she had reached the far side of the lawn, and now stood nearly at the entrance gate. I'm being foolish, she chided herself, don't let a silly old woman upset you. Get back over there and buy something for tea.

She looked around at the possibilities. It seemed that there was only one cake stall and she wasn't about to go back over there to face more confrontation, no matter how good that Dundee cake had looked.

In the distance she could see George Walker hard at work, slicing the meat from his barbecued hog. That wasn't an option either, Olive told herself, pork was definitely off the menu.

Apart from a sweet stall selling bonbons and toffees, the only other place to find a decent offering for her family was from a makeshift tent, constructed out of a washing line, four poles and a huge sheet. The sign above it read 'Fresh Pies' in childlike handwriting, with the letters sloping downwards as if the writer had run out of space near the end of the cardboard. Olive decided that a tasty pie might be something that would fill their hungry bellies and she strolled over, determined to buy something then leave.

As she approached, a familiar smell reached Olive's nostrils, sweet and sickly, just exactly as she had remembered it from some months ago. Sure enough, there was Malcolm Taft, a great clumsy hulk of a man, handing out meat pies like there was no tomorrow. Olive gagged and then panicked.

The grass seemed to move and slowly started to rise up before Olive's eyes, she turned her face upwards to try to still the sensation but now the clouds came crashing down at her. For the few seconds that Olive remained conscious, she felt as though she were being swallowed whole by some mythical beast. She was aware of strange voices around her but they seemed so far away that she was unable to hear what they were saying. She tried to move her lips to cry for help but nothing happened, her face held a strange numbness that restrained her speech and her tongue felt heavy as though it were made of lead. Olive attempted to open her eyes, the last sense to be unaffected, but they were heavy and refused to co-operate. She lay back and closed her mind, oblivious to the villagers bustling around her.

Sometime later when she awoke, Olive found herself lying stretched out on the sofa in her own living room. She had a blue woollen blanket over her that she knew was usually kept at the bottom of the ottoman, it was itchy against her bare arms. There was something cold dribbling across her eyelids so she looked up. Geoff was at her side, dabbing a cool flannel on her forehead. She tried to move.

"You just keep still", he muttered, "You've bumped your head. I never should have left you."

Olive raised her eyes upwards and a familiar face looked down at her.

"Are you alright, love?" asked Mrs. Hamilton pronouncing every syllable slowly as though she feared that Olive's brain might have been affected. However, she did look genuinely concerned.

Olive nodded. Her head was throbbing but the rest of her body didn't feel too bad. She raised her hand to touch where the pain was coming from and felt a large swelling underneath her hair. Ouch, that hurt.

"I'm alright", she muttered, "But I saw... Taft... and he was..."

"Shhh", cooed her friend, "Don't try to talk."

Mrs. Hamilton fussed with the blanket, making sure that both Olive's arms and legs were covered properly, and then lay the back of her hand on her friend's neck to see how warm she was.

'I've called the doctor, just to be on the safe side", Geoff told their neighbour, "He should be here soon. Thank you for fetching me, now you get off home and have your supper."

'I can stay if you need me to", Olive's friend smiled down at her, "I don't mind."

Olive shook her head. "You go", she whispered, sinking back down on to the pillows underneath her, all she really wanted to do was sleep without people checking on her every two minutes, and besides, it really hurt every time her husband or neighbour required her to think or answer.

"Well, if you're sure", clucked Mrs. Hamilton, picking up her handbag from the armchair next to where Olive lay on the sofa, "I've bought myself one of Malcolm's delicious meat pies to warm up."

Epilogue

Olive rocked back in her comfortable velvet-covered armchair and popped another lemon bonbon into her mouth, they'd always been her favourites and reminded her of a time long ago when she'd been a young girl. She eyed two of her grandchildren, now sitting on the green velvet sofa opposite. Olive was still fairly nimble and healthy at the grand old age of ninety-six, despite decades of smoking and drinking copious amounts of red wine. The lines on her aged face were nothing more than slight ridges and she could easily have been mistaken for a woman of some twenty years younger. She wondered what the two women on the sofa were thinking as they stared across at her.

"And that is the story of the village", Olive concluded, slapping her hands on her knees in defeat, "Now you know everything, I haven't left anything out."

The two girls, already in their forties with families of their own, looked dubiously at each other. It had taken over three hours for their grandmother to tell them about the village that she had once lived in with her young family. Now that the story was told, she looked drained.

"So when did all this happen, Nan?" one of the women asked, not really believing all of the aspects of the fantastical tale that their ageing relative had just imparted. She silently wondered whether her elderly grandma was becoming a bit senile and getting confused.

"In the early 1950's", replied Olive sadly, shaking her head as she tried to recall the exact years "Oh, I know you don't believe me. I bet you're thinking I'm losing my marbles, don't you?"

"No Nan", retorted the other woman sharply, a pretty blonde with the same shapely figure as the generations of women who had been born in to the family before her, "But it does seem a bit far-fetched."

Olive closed her eyes for a few seconds, judging the best way to handle this situation without either party getting frustrated with the other. Eventually she gave up trying to think of a tactful way to put her point across and let out a deep sigh. "It's all true", she huffed, now letting her eyes rest upon those of her incredulous grand-daughters, and waiting for a reaction, "If you don't believe me, ask your mothers. They were there you know, and what they didn't see your grandfather told them years later."

"Will they still remember?" asked the darker girl, nervously picking at the hem of her black trousers.

"Huh, I wouldn't be surprised if the very same or even worse sordid shenanigans are still going on", replied the old woman, wearily shaking her head, "I've never known a place like it."

An older lady, now entered the room with a tray of coffee mugs. She still had shaggy blonde hair despite being in her early seventies and her eyes were as blue as the sky on a clear day.

"What have I missed?" she laughed, "I've made you all a coffee."

Olive rubbed a hand across her lips, feeling quite thirsty all of a sudden "Thanks Eileen dear, do you know that I haven't touched a drop of tea since leaving the village in 1955?"

"Yes, I know mother", nodded her daughter, "You tell me every day."

"I've been telling the girls about the village", replied Olive, ignoring the last comment, "There were more strange folk in that one square mile than in the rest of the country put together."

Her daughter sighed, "Oh mother, you're right. But let it be now, won't you?"

"Where is the village?" the younger women asked in unison, now getting more and more curious.

Olive and Eileen frowned at each other, the younger woman shaking her head slightly, silently telling her mother not to say any more on the subject. Olive shrugged and reached for her drink.

"Oh, come on Aunty Eileen. Nan?" pushed the blonde, getting annoyed that she couldn't be privy to the information "There's no harm in telling us surely. We don't know anyone living there now do we?"

Eileen spluttered the coffee that she had just sipped all over the carpet. "Damn!" she yelled.

'What?" shrieked the darker woman, quite startled, "We don't do we?."

Their aunt took a deep breath. "You might do, and that's all I'm going to say about it."

"Well, who?" the dark girl countered, "Don't just leave it like that. Tell us who it is."

"Nope. Not another word on the matter, your Nan will only start getting upset."

"Well, how far away is it. At least tell us that", whined the dark girl, her thick brown curls bobbing up and down as she turned from one relative to another "We could go there and see what it's like now."

"It's closer than you would think", whispered Olive, "And much too close for comfort."

With that she closed her eyes and fell into a light afternoon nap, as was now always her custom in the middle of the afternoon.

Printed in Great Britain
by Amazon